Robbed

CL Sayers

Copyright © 2016 CL Sayers
First print edition: November 1, 2016
ISBN: 099561301X
ISBN-13: 978-0995613010

Cover design by CL Sayers
Cover and back cover images © Shutterstock @beeboys/hans engbers/Bildagentur Zoonar GmbH/Halfpoint
Cover fonts by Joe Bob Graphics and Hanoded Fonts
Edited by Spell Bound
Formatted by CP Smith

Dedication

To everyone in my life who has helped and supported me, especially my husband, my kids and my family. Thank you, this book wouldn't be possible without you all.
-May you be half an hour in heaven before the devil knows your dead.

The robbed that smiles steals something from the thief,"
-William Shakespeare **Othello** *(Act 1 Scene iii)*

Robbed

Prologue

'All sins are attempts to fill voids.'
- Simone Weil

"Oh God. Oh God. Oh God." The smell of ammonia starts to tickle and burn the back of my throat and I swear I'm going to vomit circles around myself. Just to add another level to this utter humiliation.

It's impossible to find anything to work as a light source in here, it's so dark and I have no idea when anyone is going to find me. It's a Friday, so for all I know I could be here until Monday morning. Wouldn't that just be perfect? At least the smell of ammonia might cover up the smell of my own stale piss when I finally get my freedom, 50 odd hours from now.

It mustn't be too late in the day yet because I can hear the giggles and whispers from the bitches that put me in here. I manage to feel enough room with my feet to pace all of three steps forwards and backwards, slowly wearing a path on the flooring, reminding myself that in a few short weeks I'll be out of this hell hole and finishing my education somewhere else.

The one person who had made my life here somewhat reasonable was of no use to me anymore. Why he turned on me, and why I'm now suffering through the monstrosity that is my life alone for seven hours a day, I have no idea. I can't think of that now; I have to think of something else because I'm not giving them any more of my tears. That's not true, when I do eventually get home to my own bed I'll ugly cry myself into a fitful sleep coma, but I am sure as fuck not letting them see me cry ever again.

The whispers have quietened down now. I wish I could hear better what's going on. Maybe when I know they're gone I can bang on the door and shout for help. All of a sudden the voices are getting progressively louder and aggressive.

Oh thank you sweet baby Jesus, maybe someone has worked out that the Stepford Bitches have locked me in here and I might actually get home today with my bladder intact.

There's rustling and fumbling at the door handle and finally the door swings open blinding my eyes that have just started getting used to the pitch black. When my retinas finally start to come to life again I look up into the largest pair of stormy emerald green eyes that used to mean the world to me; but now just remind me of the agony of betrayal. I manage to choke out one word before I run as fast as I can to the nearest bathroom and then to my freedom.

"Fin."

Chapter One

12 years later.

Is it even possible to put on mascara without looking like you're trying to give your first blow job? As I try to finish putting on the last of my make-up before I make my way to the bar, I decide to test the theory and realise that I now look like bloody Malcolm McDowell because I've smudged my mascara on the top and bottom of my eyelid. When will I learn not to try this crap when I'm actually trying to get somewhere on time?

After finishing the rush job of my eye makeup, there's just one thing left to do. I add my fake freckles using an eyebrow pencil, because everybody dressing up like Pink has to have the freckles, and I'm good to go.

The boys are already down at the bar getting ready for the charity karaoke night. It's been a time honoured tradition before I started lecturing at Belfast Uni when I was still an undergrad trying to manage my time between lectures, drink-a-thons and rugby matches. Now before you get all judgey on me, I am not a rugby rabbit. It's a truth universally acknowledged that a woman who wants to get laid finds herself a sportsman. Those who want to get laid a lot becomes a groupie for that sport. I was their unofficial match medic since my best friend, Mark, played hooker and my boyfriend, Robbie, was their captain. I will say, in fairness, Robbie was not my boyfriend when I started coming to administer 'magic sponges' and attempt to stop 'manic exercise with hangover' induced vomiting fits; but he is the one and only rugby player I've ever dated.

I've been involved as an unofficial member of the team for over eight years now so I'm expected to live up to these charity events as much as the next member.

● ● ●

"Right, slut, shots!" Mark so gentlemanly greets me.

"For the love of God and all that is holy, no fucking Sambuca tonight, Mark, I have a lecture to give in the morning on the joys of Elizabethan literature," I all but beg him.

"Fine, fine. You're no fun anymore. Tequila it is then." I'm actually okay with this, I think my years of regular, reasonably gentle tequila abuse has actually given me a higher tolerance to it. Mark, however, becomes not only a bigger whore on the stuff but it raises his flirting to near combustible levels.

After the requisite salt, slam, lime, Mark starts up with his recently acquired need to get me some. "So, you finally gonna hook up tonight?" None of the other players, current or former would have the balls to take me up on this, Mark only gets bragging rights because he's known me for over a decade.

"No, Mark. How many times do we have to go over this? I'm perfectly happy with my BBs and my BOB at the minute."

"Christ, why do you have to use acronyms for everything? I swear it's a fucking teacher thing. What the fuck is a BB and BOB anyways?" How can I tell that Mark has clearly been waiting here for me a while? He only drops this many f-bombs outside of his testosterone-fuelled entourage when he's already three sheets to the wind.

"My Book Boyfriend of the moment, who aptly has the initials BB, is Blake Burns, and my BOB is my Battery Operated Boyfriend. Orgasms guaranteed without the sticky mess."

"Too much information, Livvy, seriously. Jesus!" he protests. Although I do still see that tell-tale glint in his eye that every penis-wearing member of the population gets when confronted with the imagery of a non-related female masturbating.

He continues on without giving me chance for rebuttal. "It's been two years, you are eventually going to have to come out from behind your wall and actually start living again. I'm not saying you immediately go out and shack up with someone, but for the love of all that is holy at least give your vagina some human interaction outside of your hand. Your bloody hymen's going to grow back at this rate." Since Mark actually has a science-related degree I know there's no point in trying to argue the fundamental laws of biology that feat would actually break. It is, however, something in my lesser sane moments that I'm actually scared might happen; it's been that long since I got some action.

"You know, Robbie wouldn't want this, Elizabeth," he adds in a sombre half whisper.

I know he's only trying to help and he's being deadly serious by the use of my actual name, but I am not in the mood for a deep and meaningful tonight or any other night soon. "Enough! You are not going there tonight, Mark. I just want to go out, sing some angsty songs, raise a bit of money and have some fun." He wisely takes heed and waves to the bartender for another round of shots.

I step back from the bar, pleased to see that the rugby club's fundraiser has attracted quite a turn out. Even through the dim overhead lights of the bar I can see the kaleidoscope of disco lights bouncing off an eclectic mix of costumes. There's signage everywhere advertising the suicide prevention charity that the rugby club has chosen to sponsor this year. It's a cause close to many of the students at Belfast University, given the strain a lot of people find themselves under, whether it's from their own thoughts and expectations or those thrust on them by well-meaning friends and family members.

As Mark saunters by to put our names in to the karaoke MC I'm smacked across the face by the full effect of his costume. As the only bi-sexual member of the university rugby team, people might expect Mark to tone himself down. Not my best friend. He's been this way since we met at 16. What you see is what you get and if you don't like it – don't let the door hit you on the ass on your way out. Tonight he looks like a cross between Freddie Mercury and the biker from YMCA. All leather and facial hair, but you have to appreciate the way the leather sculpts his shoulders and shows off the cut of his tight ass.

We're only a couple of drinks into the night when I hear my name being called through the microphone. I've become a regular at these, not because of a Beyoncé-style voice or anything, just because I'll always do what I can to support Mark and the boys, even if it means dressing up and making a fool out of myself.

I hear the familiar opening chords to "Just Like a Pill", my standard karaoke fodder and ready myself with a few breaths. Without looking at the words, I use the music and the lyrics as a catharsis, one of the few times I allow myself to really feel, I know it adds to the sound of my voice but that's not why I do it. It may seem strange, but up on stage I can allow myself to feel. To grieve. To hope and to wallow. Because I know after the song finishes, I step away from the mic and the stage. Everything closes back up again into its neat little box where I can contain, control and ignore its very existence.

Through the coda, I allow myself a moment to scan the room, seeing friendly, supportive and some all too knowing faces. I catch Mark and see him talking to someone who could be God's gift to women if his face is as beautiful as his body. Dressed as Doctor Who, from the long beige trench coat to the blue suit and tatty red converse trainers. If he's wearing the black-rimmed glasses, I may have a small orgasm on stage in front of 300 people.

When he turns away from Mark and locks eyes with me, I'm thankful I know this song the same way I can remember the hymns that were drummed into me in school, because it's not the glasses that freezes the marrow in my bones and causes all the blood to rush from my face. It's his face – a face I haven't seen in over a decade, except in my nightmares.

Chapter Two

What the fuck is he doing here? Why the fuck is he talking to Mark of all people? Does he know who I am now? Has the life I've meticulously constructed for myself the last 12 years been for nothing? If he's here then there may be others too, and as strong as I like to think I am, I cannot deal with coming face to face with more than one ghost from my past at a time.

No, of course he won't recognise me. I'm determined to reason with myself. He couldn't possibly recognise me. It was 12 years and 60 lbs ago. I've worked hard to become the person I am. When I left St Ignacious and met Mark, he helped me start finding other ways to deal with stress other than eating. Primarily going to martial arts classes that were free in our Liberal Arts school and any free class that was running at our local gym. By cutting out the comfort eating and using exercise to take the edge off my anxiety, I started to lose weight. I liked the way I looked when I started to lose weight, so I started dieting properly. Carefully counting my calorie intake and working out just how many miles and what pace I needed to run to burn off the calories I'd eaten and perhaps a few more for good measure. It felt good to not be the girl that was nicknamed 'beached whale' anymore. Once I started losing the weight properly, I obviously needed a new haircut to match, a nice short pixie style, and my glasses didn't match my new hairstyle so I got contacts. It's unbelievable the extent that that amount of weight loss can change your whole face and body shape.

It's been a long time since I stood in front of the mirror and compared the old and new me, but I am certain he couldn't recognise me now. I worked hard to become the new me that people couldn't walk over and hurt.

As I slowly make my way towards the bar and my uncertain future, I thought I saw a flash of recognition in his eyes but in a fleeting second it was gone again.

"Livvy, love. You have to meet my new *friend!*" Mark declares so loudly I'm sure the guy on stage, who looks like the singer from LMFAO, heard him.

"Hey, I'm Livvy?" I didn't mean to phrase it like a question and judging by his perfectly raised eyebrow and half smirk, he caught it too. *Great way to make a lasting first impression, dumbass.*

"Fin, nice to meet you." His voice has changed over time. I hadn't been expecting that, in my head and in my dreams he was still the 16-year-old boy who broke my heart and threw me to the wolves in one calculated move that no matter how many times I dreamed about, I still couldn't understand.

"Fin's my new partner." Mark is practically vibrating with glee, nodding and grinning at me as if I should understand what the hell he means. Was Fin gay? Was that why he turned on me?

"Congratulations, you didn't tell me you'd found the one, Mark," I reply, noticing Fin choke on his mouthful of Guinness.

"Don't be so bloody stupid, Olivia, he's my new partner at the paper!" Then he added with a wink, "Although you know if you swung my way I wouldn't kick you out of bed for snoring, Fin." Fin returns his comment with a flirty smile and a smooth laugh, dashing my hopes that his closeted sexuality had been the reasoning behind his betrayal.

Part of me can't help but feel insulted by the fact that he either doesn't remember or recognise me, yet I spotted him straight away. It just adds to my ire that obviously he meant much more to me, my life and my survival, than I ever did to him.

Mark pulls me away from my own thoughts by spotting one of his regulars. Mark is very much a free-love type of person, he doesn't believe his love should be tied down to one person, of any sex; he has plenty of love to go around.

"I see someone who's going to keep me company tonight, back in a mo." And off he sweeps, parting the crowd like the Dead Sea, his target set on the tall, blonde suit with the man bun. With nowhere else to look, I have to turn back around, facing Fin and my past.

"So, you're working with Mark, are you a reporter too?" May as well ease myself into this situation, but in the time it takes him to answer I get a much better look at him and his outfit.

While I shrunk down over the past ten years, Fin appears to have filled out quite well. He fills the blue pinstripe suit as if it were made for him and from the shape of his body that I can make out under his crisp, white shirt, he's obviously kept up with the competitive-level swimming he began in school. His biceps bulge as he lifts his glass to his lips, taking a drink, darting his tongue out to swipe at the creamy froth covering his top lip. God, how can he look even better now that he is clearly a man? I need to get a grip of myself, physical attraction doesn't mean a thing when you know you can't trust him as far as you can throw him. And given that he's at least six inches taller and a hell of a lot of muscle mass bigger than me, that's not very far.

He's managed to make the ultimate nerd-style look amazing. The black rim of his glasses drawing attention to the perfect emerald shade of his eyes, framed by his dark eyelashes. The one button of his suit that he's fastened pulls your eyes to his trim waist, which is in complete contrast to his broad shoulders which are just shy of straining and hulking out against the suit's seams which are making a brave effort to control and clothe his body.

His eyes seem to be assessing me as he swallows his drink and places the glass back on the bar. "No, I'm a photographer. I'll be working with Mark on a few specific pieces the paper has lined up. And what is it you do exactly?"

"I'm a lecturer at Belfast University, English and Irish Literature."

"Are you one of those people who just studies and dissects art rather than appreciating it?"

"No, I've actually written a couple of books myself. One fiction, one non-fiction. I appreciate art as art, but I also like to give my students the skills to dissect and analyse as needed. Did I pass the test?" I don't know why this is rubbing me the wrong way, but I don't like people criticising my job, I've worked damned hard to get where I am today.

"You passed with flying colours. I like the idea of appreciating and understanding art at the same time. It wouldn't be right to just pick apart the piece of someone's soul they've put on display. Do ya know what I mean?"

It's hard not to notice a southern brogue to his accent that was never there before, but I'm not sure whether to mention it or not. I don't know how long it'll be until he realises who I am – if he ever does. I decide it would probably be more suspect not to mention the fact that I notice his accent isn't entirely local. "Have you just moved up here? I couldn't help but notice your accent." God, was my voice actually as breathy as it sounded in my own head? *Do not flirt with this man! You know better!*

"You spotted that, did ya? I just moved up from Dublin last week, I've been wanting to come back up North for a while but I was waiting for a permanent job to open up."

"Oh, have you lived in Dublin for long?"

"I moved down there as soon as I finished high school. Worked for my degree and then found different bits and pieces of work while I also freelanced. It was a good experience, I even got to photograph at ComicCon last year." The way he adds this last bit of information on is almost as if he's testing me, I mean who hasn't heard of ComicCon? *We'll just see about that.*

"Really, is that where you got your David Tennant inspiration from?" I drop the Doctor Who name in and watch his eyes widen for a second before I go in for the kill, "But then again, you're too young to pull off William Hartnell and you don't have the hair for Patrick Troughton." I smile sweetly at him while he just stares intently at me, with a look on his face I can't quite read. His voice is rough and scratchy when he replies, "Marry me."

I somehow manage to avoid choking on my drink in response to his declaration. *Right, time to shut this down.* I need to remember who this is. It doesn't matter how good looking or funny he is, he's still the one person you thought you could trust and who left you completely alone when you needed him most. Time to extract yourself from this bizarre situation. I mean he's working with Mark, it's not like you're going to become best friends again. Just keep it casual and walk away.

I look up, and up – *jeez, what height is he?* His eyes seem to have darkened to more of a hazel, and I fight the pull to get lost there. I toss the rest of my drink back and start to walk away, secretly headed towards the back bar to keep drinking, and call over my shoulder, "Nice to meet you, Flynn!"

Just before I'm out of hearing distance I hear him call back with a laugh in his voice, "You know, it's Fin."

Chapter Three

Someone make it stop. I try to scramble back under the covers to escape the constant shrieking from my clock. Poking one eye out I survey the carnage that lays before me. Abandoned clothes? Check. Make up still on face? Ugh. Check. Curtains still wide open for the world to look in? Creepy check. Did I at least remember to take my contacts out? Blurry, check.

Using herculean strength, I drag my sorry ass to the bathroom, thumping my alarm clock on the way, to try and pass as human for my class. I don't want to give myself a heart attack so I deliberately avoid the mirror when I grab my meds from the cupboard, wash them down and jump into the shower.

An hour and two cups of coffee later, I grab my messenger bag and make my way to the bus stop. Settling into a window seat I watch all the Freshers walk by, some making the inevitable walk of shame. As much as I try to avoid the thought process, the green fields and shrubbery whizzing past remind me of the green eyes that have haunted me for the past 12 years.

I allow myself the bus journey to think and wallow, and after that I resolve to put him back in his box. I think back to last night, as strong as I want to be I can't think back to the Fin I remember from before that. The strong cut of his muscles that were hinted at through his suit rather than blatantly on display. His tousled, mahogany hair that looks like he's made a half-hearted attempt to faux-hawk it. He either didn't realise or care that half the men and women in the bar tracked his every movement with lust-filled eyes. No matter how many years have passed he still has those heart-shaped lips. He used to hate them, thought they were too feminine.

Before I can stop myself I start to wonder if he stills feels that way. I remember how they felt when they were pressed up against mine; soft, yet unyielding, just the right amount of pressure to spark pressure elsewhere in my body. That's my cue to stop reminiscing because I won't – can't – go back down that road. I've had enough kicks to the teeth now to know not to court it too.

Just as I forcibly remove myself from my own thoughts the bus pulls up at my stop. I double check the time on my phone and see I have just enough time for a third caffeine hit, which will undoubtedly make me less likely to lose my mind at my students.

• • •

Several hours, coffees and inane questions later, I finally get to finish up my last class of the day. Thank the Lord today was only a half day's teaching. As I bend down to pick up my bag I hear footsteps shuffling towards me. I'm not surprised when I look up and see Steve hovering, his bloodshot eyes desperately trying to stay focused on one point. Every time I look at this dude he reminds me of Silent Bob, and not just because he always smells like weed.

Steve lingers around until he manages to communicate, sans words, that he wants to hand in an extra credit paper. I swear I don't get paid enough to put up with this shit. I finally get to check my phone and see that Mark is waiting for me at the café down the street. Food. Yes, food is what my body needs at this point. Any more caffeine and I'm likely to start vibrating.

Thankfully, I'm only a few minutes' walk away from greasy food and pastries, but I'll probably have to make up for it the rest of this week. It's not often I indulge myself, but a raging hangover is definitely one of those times. I manage to weave my way through the plethora of students, teachers and nine-to-fivers making their way for lunch. Spotting Mark at a window seat, I move towards him, noticing that he's already got my favourite hangover lunch sitting in front of him waiting for me to devour it. God bless that beautiful man.

When you're ridiculed for years for being plus-sized (read "fat bitch") you tend to get a bit sensitive about what you eat. So, you know I've gone really heavy on the drink if I'm about to pound a plate full of carbs into me.

Plopping my fat ass down onto a seat, Mark nudges the plate towards me as if he can see the crazy ready to come out and wants to placate the beast ready to rear its hungover head.

"Ssooooo…" my head snaps up at Mark's not so subtle attempt to start a conversation before I even have food in my stomach. I make a noise at him that would imply he should continue; I'd never testify to it in court but there's a chance it *may* have been a grunt. What can I say? I don't do hangry. Don't judge.

"Ssooo…" I repeat, making the universal get-the-hell-on-with-it wrist roll.

"So, what did you think of Fin? You two seemed to hit it off. You know, he was asking about you this morning." I can feel myself shaking my head before he's even finished his sentence.

"Nope. Nuh uh, not starting this here." I sit back in my chair to reinforce just how much I'm not willing to try and discuss Fin Kelly in a public place or with a banging hangover. Thank God I only had a half day of teaching. There's a real chance I would've ripped his damn head off otherwise.

"Fine. But you're not getting away that easily, I want details and I will get them tonight, missy." Mark mimics my position and promptly throws a French fry at me, effectively punctuating his point and dissipating any tension before it had a chance to build.

I realise that really, this is a fruitless argument and he won't let it go until he finds out what's going on. Maybe it wouldn't be a bad thing to share this with him. He already knows all about Fin. Hell, he was the one who helped to put me back together when I came trudging in from St Ignacious' all those years ago, every inch of my body covered in baggy clothes and my hair covering my face. Mark could give me some perspective on this whole messed up situation.

Having agreed to spill all at dinner we go back to usual form and discuss Mark's conquest of the evening. Mark managed to get tall, blonde and suited to take him home last night, he's apparently called Michael and unfortunately for Mark, everything wasn't in proportion so he was left more than a little disappointed.

"It's false advertising if you look like that and don't have the goods to back it up. I mean, if he at least knew what he was doing with it I could work with that. It was like he was trying to play the hokey pokey," he finishes his rant with a huff and slumps back into his seat.

"Can't say I've ever had that problem, Mark, but I'm sure you showed him exactly where he was going wrong." I try, and fail to hide the smirk tugging at my lips.

"Is it too much to ask to find a guy or girl who doesn't have to be shown exactly what to do and can let me take control without feeling like I'm teaching a class?"

"And that right there is where I bow out of this conversation. You talk about class and sex in the same sentence when I'm just finished teaching a class full of horny 19-year-olds and I'm out." I start to push my chair back and confirm our details for tonight, "Make sure you message Josie and fill her in."

"This must be big if you're bringing in reinforcements." Mark's eyebrows come close to reaching his hairline he raises them that far.

"Just...just make sure you let her know," I reply as I grab my stuff and make my way home to try and sort my head out.

• • •

I lie back on my sofa hoping the rhythmic kicking of my legs over the armrest will knock some sense or idea of how to deal with this clusterfuck in my head. Of course, I don't have that sort of luck. Thankfully, Mark and Josie should be here soon so they can either talk me down from this mental ledge or at least wallow with me.

I answer the knock on my door to Mark looking his usual dashing self, wearing low-slung jeans and an Ulster rugby jersey. Mark seems to be as comfortable in a rugby jersey as he is in his birthday suit; he was born to wear both. Josie follows close behind in wedge heels and a long, flowing skirt. She's really digging her hippy-chic vibe at the minute, as evidenced by the flower headband she's rocking too.

Throwing herself down onto a chair and cracking open a bottle of Corona, she immediately starts her interrogation, "So, what's happening that we've had to convene the coven?"

As Mark makes sure the beers are safely ensconced in the fridge and situates himself; I start filling Josie in on the events from the night before.

"So, what's the big deal? A hot guy, that Mark is lucky enough to get to work with, lucky bitch, shows an interest in you. How is this a calamity, exactly?" Barely taking a breath she manages to continue, "I know what happened with Rob left you more than a little gun-shy, but maybe this is a sign that you should…"

"A little gun-shy? A little gun-shy!" I can't stop myself from interrupting her, "My boyfriend was killed, no strike that, my *fiancé* was killed, because you know what Josie, that's exactly what he would've been if some moron hadn't thought it was a good idea to get hammered and then drive his own drunk ass home!" I increase my grip on my bottle to try and calm down the shaking in my hands. Realising I'm taking my frustrations out on my best friends, I much more softly continue, "So forgive me for being *a little* gun-shy."

Mark and Josie share a look that I've come to know too well as they sit back and wait for the storm and threatened tears to pass. Taking a deep breath, I explain the crux of my current problem to them both. "It's not about being gun-shy, and it's not about desecrating Rob's memory." I blow out a breath hoping for some courage, "it's about Elizabeth McKeen."

Concern and confusion mar both their features as Mark asks the inevitable question, "What does this have to do with your old name in high school, Livvy?"

"Mark, you know the whole story of what I was like and what I went through in St Ignacious before I started at BCLA, but I never gave you details."

"You gave me more than enough detail of what those bottom feeders did to you, Livvy, I can't think what other details you could possibly give." My Mark, as always, giving me support even when I don't realise I need it.

Josie chips in, "The Stepford Bitches making your life a living hell, you ending up medicated, alone and in a brand new school. But what does any of this have to do with a hot new photographer at Mark's paper?"

"You both remember how I had one person, one solitary person that helped me through it all. Kept me sane, kept me from doing something so stupid and irrational, that I can't even believe I considered it. You both also know that one day he just," *God, would these words ever get any easier?* "He just stopped. Stopped helping me, supporting me, loving me. He threw me to the wolves and as if that wasn't bad enough, he started joining in. He would just stand there watching, waiting to see what they would do or say next. Well, um, what I never told you was his name. I couldn't – can't – bring myself to think about him because it hurts my heart, every time. But back then I would've sworn on any holy book you put in front of me that he was my soulmate." A harsh, bitter laugh that I don't recognise as my own escapes my lips. "How naïve was I? I thought I was so lucky to have found him so young. Fintan Joseph Kelly was my absolute everything, until one day he just…wasn't."

The crash of Mark's bottle against the table wrenches me out of my own thoughts, and I realise that by only thinking about myself and my own history I've probably triggered the anger that Mark has worked so hard to control.

"Motherfucker." He spits his vitriol with every harshly barked word, as he paces my living room floor. "I. Will. Fucking. End. Him."

"Mark, don't, please." I pace alongside him hoping that if he sees me calm, it will help to calm the emotions I can feel threatening to explode. Grabbing both his hands I force him to come to a stop and look me in the eyes, "Mark, it was a long time ago. I've moved on. If I hadn't gone through that, I never would've gone to BCLA and I never would've met you." I will him to feel the truth in my words, to let go of the anger. I know from experience it's not that easy, but I hope he can see that him being upset is doing nothing but upsetting me. He also needs to calm down and release my hands if I'm to have any hope of getting the blood to flow back through them again.

Josie calmly comes over and takes Mark's face in her hands, she gently turns his head so he's looking her in the eyes. She shushes him and just keeps repeating in a soft voice, "It's okay, you're calm." Whatever Mark voodoo she seems to behold, is working because slowly but surely Mark's breathing calms and he breaks eye contact to look at me and ask what I want to do about the situation.

Chapter Four

After another couple of beers, we've all relaxed enough to try and broach the subject of Fin again. "What do you want to do about this, Livvy? It's clear he doesn't recognise you. No one could be that much of a wanker to push for a date with you after everything he did." Mark punctuates his point by necking the last of his bottle.

"What can I do? I'll just tell him I'm not interested and move on." To me it seems like the most rational way of dealing with it.

"Yeah, honey, I don't think that'll work." Josie throws in. "He's either going to think you're playing hard to get or it's going to make any interaction you do have even more awkward. If he's going to be working with Mark as much as it seems, you're going to have a lot of interactions or have to stop seeing Mark until Fin decides to move on to the next job."

Interrupting Josie in her tracks Mark throws another spanner in the works, "That's *if* he moves on to another job darling, from what I've heard from the higher-ups, they want to 'make Fin an offer he can't refuse'." Proving once again that Mark, no matter how much drink he's imbibed, cannot pull off a Mafioso accent.

Ugh, this is exactly my luck. Just as I find myself finding my new normal I have to try to get the strength and will to climb over yet another stumbling block.

"Oookkkaayy, then it's simple. We make it so Fin *wants* to find a new job." Clearly pleased with her evil genius idea, Josie slouches back on her chair with a grin that distinctly reminds me of the cat from Alice in Wonderland. This does not bode well for the rest of this conversation. Apparently not drunk enough to miss Mark and I's expectant looks waiting for her to elaborate, she leans forward with her serious face on and braces both her elbows on her knees. "It's straightforward and actually it kills two birds with one stone. A stone that is in serious need of some hard, fast, repetitive buffing." Cue the Vaudeville eyebrow raise, "So, Livvy agrees to go on a date with Fin. She waxes, preens and polishes herself and does her best femme fatale routine. She makes the twisted little fucker fall madly in love with her and doles out a little karma. She breaks his heart, shows him how uncomfortable life would be here if he stuck around and voila: one asshole bully surgically removed, no muss, no fuss."

• • •

All three of us sit up until the early hours of the morning, alternating shots of vodka with more beer, perfecting the plan of how I, "Bessie the Elephant" McKeen, is somehow going to seduce my former best friend, make him fall in love with me and then break his heart. The break his heart thing I think I can manage, all I have to do is cast my mind back to those last few months of high school, or hell, look in my medicine cabinet at the pharmacy of anti-anxiety and anti-depressant meds I have stocked in there and I should have enough fuel to feed my anger and hurt.

It's the thought of having to allow this, this man back into my life. To open myself up, even if it's under disguise, and let him in enough that he'll fall in love with me. The riskiest part of this is if I *can* seduce him and somehow smokescreen him enough to make him fall in love with me. Given that he's on the very short list of people who have truly gotten to see and know the real me and then he clearly found me lacking, doesn't fill me with confidence.

There is one specific perk though. I remember the Fin I used to love. I remember the Fin I used to sit and make out with under the stars. I remember the Fin, who even at 18 was gorgeous and built, and from what I felt poking me in the stomach all those years ago would be a very big way to break myself back in. It doesn't take much in my drink-fogged brain to remember the Fin of last night. His even taller form, to the point that my 5'5" height barely brings me to his collarbone. His messy mop of mahogany hair that curls in just at the bottom of his ears, barely touching his collar. His broad shoulders that taper down to his hips, the epitome of the perfect swimmer's body that I have no doubt belies his true strength. All the perfect physical attributes for providing me with my first non-self-provided orgasms in over two years.

It may be the beer and vodka talking but this sounds like a hell of a good plan.

Chapter Five

A few days later at too-fucking-early on a Saturday morning, I have myself wrapped up warm to make my way to the BelU rugby pitches. I started out as a fill-in field medic when I was a lowly fresher and after I started dating Robbie, became a part of the furniture. I have my travel mug of sweet, heavenly coffee in one hand and my medical bag in the other. We're playing one of the rougher teams today so I've a funny feeling my medical bag is going to come in handy.

I'm already set up and ready to go at the side of the pitch when I hear Josie grumbling as she walks up to take her position beside me, not that she actually helps with anything, she just likes to have a close view of the men in tight shorts. "It's too bloody early and cold for this bollocks. Stupid fucking Mark, stupid fucking rugby."

"Oh shut up, Josie. You know you love it. You wouldn't be here otherwise." I'm not in the mood to placate her when I'm standing here freezing my nipples off waiting on the game to start.

There's a decent crowd assembled today, probably because we're playing on our home pitch. Even when I'm cold and tired the vibe emanating from the crowd invigorates me. We haven't lost a match yet and with the university threatening to remove our subsidisation after this year, it's important that we move up in the league. The more attention and publicity we can draw, the less likely the university will want the negative press of removing our funding.

The deafening roar of clapping and shouting alerts me to the boys running out onto the pitch. I can see Mark running out with his game face on, for such a good looking man he looks like he could fuck you up if you look at him the wrong way when he's in game mode. While Mark makes his way to centre pitch, the rest of the team assume a huddle of their half of the pitch. A familiar head of hair draws my eye away from the coin toss. Holy mother of Jesus, Fintan fucking Kelly is standing yards away from me in a pair of short shorts. I can actually see the definition in his thigh muscles and my tongue wants to lead me to them. *Bad tongue, bad, bad tongue.*

I can think of no Earthly reason why Fin is on the field right now, I can also think of no reason why Mark, may he rest in peace – cause I'm going to fucking kill him – wouldn't warn me about this.

The bastard sees that I'm watching him and has the cheek to wink at me. I resist the urge to give him a one-fingered salute and remember that I'm supposed to be trying to lure him to me. I need to remember that we are at the beginning of Operation Karma. Yes, I know, not the most original title but it's difficult to come up with something better when there's more alcohol than blood flowing through your body. So instead, I give him a timid smile, turn towards Josie and give wide eyes hoping that she receives my telepathic scream for help.

As any good friend should, she gets my message loud and clear and looks over my shoulder to the huddle. "It's all good, he's joined the huddle, you can return to your normally scheduled programming now."

I can see today turning into a complete clusterfuck. In fact, it's pretty much confirmed when I take a look at the opposition. This isn't another university team, this is a group of farmers who are all built like brick shithouses and I'd hazard a guess that they've got a high pain threshold, given that some of them are using electrical tape wrapped around their ears and head to protect their ears from the scrum.

We win the coin toss and from there the pitch is a flurry of activity. The boys are really on form today and aren't letting the farmers make much headway. It really is some feat, given that some of the opposition look like they could easily deadlift one of their own cows. Aaron, a pupil in my modern literature class, ends up being brought down by a high tackle. A traffic cone would be more use on the pitch today than this referee, we've only been playing for about 15 minutes and I've already seen quite a few dubious tackles. Poor Aaron becomes a human pancake as about four burly rugby players land on top of him trying to get the ball forward. Fin speeds past me like a man possessed and starts shouldering people off Aaron, eventually the ref pulls his head from out of his ass and calls for a scrum.

Scrums are my favourite and most hated part of the game. There's something enthralling about watching eight athletic men lock shoulders and use their entire body to force another eight men to step backwards no more than a few feet. The grunts and growls of the men have me rubbing my thighs together; it's impossible not to get turned on watching all that testosterone and virility being displayed in front of you.

I can hear Fin's roars and shouts as he urges on the rest of the pack. A few seconds later and the white prize is at Fin's feet. He snatches it quickly and starts to dart around the scrum. He easily twists and turns past their first flanker, the guy catches nothing but air and Fin is speeding down the pitch. From my vantage point I can see one of their props making a beeline for Fin. Props are the front line of the scrum, by definition they 'prop up' the rest of the scrum taking the full, brutal force of everyone's momentum. They are huge. Like Bruce Banner pissed off, huge. This man-mountain is barrelling towards Fin and it looks like he's going to make a direct intercept. Fin is too busy looking between the try line and the other player chasing him up his right hand side, he doesn't see the human wall that's about to collide with him.

I unconsciously grab Josie's hand just as the inevitable happens. There's a huge gouge in the pitch where Fin and the prop collide and then the prop just keeps going. He comes to a stop a few feet from where he stopped dead Fin's attempt at a try. He stands up and shakes his head, as I wait, holding my breath for Fin to stand up too. I don't even realise I've grabbed Josie's hand until she squeezes it. When I look at her I can see she's speaking, but I'm not sure what she's saying because all I can hear is ringing in my ears. It lasts only a second. She repeats at me, giving me a worried look, "He's not getting up, Livvy, you need to go over there."

As I grab my bag and run over the pitch, not even looking to avoid the crevices and hollows from the day's play, the players all step back for me, creating a disconcerting guard of honour directing me to the body lying prone on the cold earth. I feel my blood run cold when I see that Fin isn't moving. He hasn't just had the wind knocked out of him, he's actually unconscious and I find myself muttering a prayer and an oath under my breath that he hasn't managed to be seriously injured.

I perform my usual techniques to try and rouse him and I notice a flinch. I shout in both ears once more and notice him starting to come round. He locks eyes with me, tries to sit up and ask, "What time is it?"

I can't contain the snort laugh that breaks free, I'm going to say it's from his bizarre reaction and not from the fact that he's actually okay. I quickly get him to lie back down while I check over him. Once I'm convinced he hasn't broken anything, I let him get up and walk him over to the sideline where Josie is standing, twisting her hands together. When she sees us hobbling over towards her, you can see the stress leave her body. That's just Josie, she openly admits to hating Fin for what he did to me, but she would never wish anybody physical harm.

While the match plays on behind me with one of the subs filling in Fin's position, I try to clean the nasty cut above his eyebrow. I will my hands to stop shaking, but it's not made any easier when Fin looks up through his lashes and smirks at me. When I try to reach for his eyebrow with antiseptic his fingers close around my wrist and I'm shocked by the heat penetrating through to my bones. "Go out with me." His voice is raspy but not harsh. When I don't answer straight away he gives my wrist a short squeeze ensuring he has my attention and repeats, "Go out with me. Tonight."

I'm pretty certain that at this point I'm doing an amazing goldfish impression because even though this was what I wanted, needed, to happen in order to start my plan for vengeance, when actually presented with the opportunity I'm at a loss for words.

I manage to force myself to nod and I think my facial muscles are listening to me when I tell them to smile. "What are you doing here, Fin?"

"So you do remember my name. Huh. Well I think, and I might be mistaken but, I think I'm playing rugby."

"Hardy, fucking, har har, Fin, I can see that you're playing rugby. My question is, why are you playing rugby for a university team that you don't attend?"

"Well, Mark was telling me about the team needing to succeed this year in the league and I've played a bit of rugby in my time, and I'm fucking awesome at it, so I thought I'd help out. The newspaper co-sponsors the rugby team with the university; so technically, I'm eligible to play for them." He shrugs his shoulders after he's finished as if that was the most normal sentence in the world.

"You're so modest. So wait, you're a ringer?" my voice manages to reach a pitch that only canines are going to be able to understand.

"Shh, keep it down will ye, it's not a public announcement!" he admonishes me and glances behind me at the pitch. "Am I all set?"

Given that I've been able to see his eyes roaming all over me and he's not slurring his words I'm gonna say that concussion isn't a worry. "You're good to go," I say while stepping away from him.

"Perfect, see you tonight," he winks at me and struts back onto the pitch. I can't help but watch his ass as he runs over to take position, his shorts fitting him snugly, showing off just how muscular he is. God I love this game.

Chapter Six

'Nothing is so good as it seems beforehand.'
- Mary Ann Evans (George Eliot)

I've managed to squeeze myself into a pair of spanx that quite frankly at this point I'm convinced should be in the Geneva convention as a form of torture. My boobs feel like they're resting somewhere up near my chin I've hoisted them up that far in this push-up bra. Here's a hint, if you're already rocking a D cup and you then wear a push-up bra you're just asking to give yourself two black eyes.

I've poured myself into a pair of skinny jeans and matched it with a hunter-green tunic cinched in at the waist with a leather belt. A trick that I picked up when I first started losing weight, it seems to give the illusion of having an hourglass figure, I still carry a fair bit of weight and some habits are hard to break no matter how much time passes.

My contacts are in and my eyeliner wings match so all I have to do now is sit down and chug several glasses of wine in quick succession to try to kill off the swarm of bees doing a conga line in my stomach.

I'm just finishing my second sip of my wine when there's a knock on my door. *Of course he couldn't be late and give me time to get some Dutch courage.* Begrudgingly I go to let him in and just catch my jaw before it lands at my feet on the floor. The man is trying to kill me, he has to be. Standing in front of me wrapped in a pair of jeans and an olive-green shirt that hugs his chest, the sleeves rolled up to his elbows show off some serious forearm action. The colour of his shirt seems to draw even more attention to his eyes which are definitely more on the green side of the scale today.

God it hurts to just look at him. How can this gorgeous man be the weasel that took the easy way out so long ago? I remember what it felt like to kiss and touch him when we were only teenagers, I can't even try to stop my mind wandering to what he would feel like underneath my fingertips now that he is so much bigger and stronger. I also realise that I've been standing in front of him blocking the doorway and I've been so lost in my head, mentally feasting on him, that I've no idea how long has passed. I step away from the door and indicate with my wine glass that he should come on in.

I make my way into the kitchen, thankful that the whole house isn't open plan so I can rest myself up against the fridge and try to collect my senses from where they've scattered all across the floor. A creak on the floor snaps my head to the right and I see Fin watching me with a bemused look on his face. Stepping up to me he asks, "Are ya okay?"

"Yes, fine. It's just been a while since I've done this." There's no point in trying to maintain my cool since he's seen me freaking out already.

Taking both my hands and turning me so I have to look at him he asks, "How long's a while?"

"Two years."

He's polite enough to only raise his eyebrows, whether he can sense I don't want to talk about it anymore or he's leaving the interrogation until later, he just nods once and announces, "let's go."

Fin drives us into Belfast city centre and I spend approximately 99.9% of the journey trying to not look like I am watching him out of the corner of my eye. (I completely am.) After parking his car, he makes a point of getting around to my side of the car to open the door for me before I have much of a chance to do it myself. He's either an absolute gentleman or laying it on pretty thick.

I look around and realise that we're in the Cathedral Quarter of Belfast. I love this area, in fact, our rival, Northern Ireland University, have a campus here. This part of Belfast is steeped in history, an almost ethereal touch as we walk the side streets. Modern and historical mingling together so that we pass several old buildings that are now social hives but maintain their original architectural facades.

We come to a stop behind St Anne's Cathedral and I realise where it is he's taking me for dinner. There's a reason why this part of Belfast is considered the cultural quarter and with the MAC theatre just a few minutes away, this area is bursting with enough restaurants to satisfy the craving of any gastronomic speciality. However, the one Fin has chosen is one of my favourites. They're famed for only ever using locally sourced, in season food, so their menu changes regularly depending on what they've got in from the local farmers. I wouldn't be surprised to come in one day and find pigs' hooves being used as napkin holders; they are the epitome of waste not, want not.

When we step inside, my senses are immediately assaulted by different noises, smells and colours. There's hand drawn illustrations on the tiles decorating the walls and all the tables and chairs are different colours and styles. It's eclectic decoration on steroids.

As we're shown to our seats, Fin follows the server and takes my hand in his so that I'm following him. It could be that fact that I haven't been on a date since Robbie died, but it warms me to know that he wants to know I'm there with him, that I'm safe.

When he pulls out my chair for me I realise that this is normal behaviour, he's not pretending. I don't think he even registers that he's doing it. I remember not seeing much of his mum in school. I always got the impression she worked a lot because she was always busy, so it was Fin's dad I got to know better. He was always very nice and kind to me, so I can only assume he's the one who taught Fin how to be such a gentleman.

Fin explains to the server that he wants to sit beside me rather than across from me. After giving the server his signature smirk, he nods and begins to rearrange the setting. Thank God the server is a man, and I can only assume straight, because anyone else would be a puddle of goo after being on the receiving end of that smirk; I know, I've been there.

Even the tableware is eclectic with not a piece of cutlery or glass matching. It should be offensive to the eyes but somehow it all blends together in a way that works. It's a kind of 'we don't give a single fuck' chic.

Fin swaps around his cutlery so his knife is on the left and his fork is on the right. Quirking my eyebrow, I ask, "are you a closet lefty, Fin?"

He replies, gracing me with his smirk, *seriously that look could never get old.* "No, it's just a quirk I picked up at some point. Apparently I was ambidextrous when I was little and I guess the cutlery part sort of stuck." He settles himself at the table and turns slightly so he's looking directly at me. "I didn't get a chance to tell you at your house how beautiful you look tonight, Livvy. Thank you for saying yes, I get the impression this isn't something you agree to often." Fin's eyes shine brightly in the candlelight and I can't help but admire and be somewhat jealous of how put together he looks. His eyelashes are practically longer than mine and they frame his jade eyes beautifully. How is it fair that a man already this good looking has eyelashes I would certainly maim, if not kill for?

"It's not as if you gave me much of chance to say 'no' now, is it?"

He reaches out and takes my hand running his thumb back and forth across my pulse point and I can't contain the sharp intake of breath from the heat in this hand and his eyes.

"I know you feel this too, Livvy. There's no way you would say no to me, to this. The chemistry between us is undeniable." He states this as if it's fact, and in a way, it is. Even if we didn't have our past I wouldn't be able to deny the intensity of our chemistry. He nods at what he must take as my unspoken agreement and lifts up his menu. His other hand, however, moves from mine, allowing me to pick up my own menu, and comes to rest on my thigh just at the hem of my tunic.

Concentrating on my menu is practically impossible because Fin keeps squeezing my thigh every so often and I'm torn between wiggling in my seat to give myself some relief from the fire he's stoking in me and moving my thigh away from him so he can't get too good a feel of just how chunky I am.

His hand remains there even as the server comes back over to take our order. I know I speak and I know it must be English because I'm not getting bizarre looks from everyone but I couldn't honestly tell you what the hell I just ordered because Fin has moved his hand so it's no longer on the top of my thigh but now on the inside and just a few scant inches would put his hand right where I want it, where he would undoubtedly be able to feel just how wet he's managed to make me with nothing more than a touch and a look.

I have a couple of glasses of red wine with dinner, but after his beer at the start of the meal, Fin moves on to water. I'm actually surprised how easily the conversation flows. Given how out of practice I am, Fin manages to make me feel at ease. But I need to remember, remind myself who Fin is. He was supposed to be my person, my sole friend who protected me and gave me solace. Until he stopped. No warning. No explanation. Nothing.

Trying to convince Fin that I'm interested isn't a difficult feat. Physically, he's even more attractive now that he's grown up and filled out. I need to be very careful right now. I can feel myself slipping back. Warming to the Fin in front of me now would be a very stupid mistake. Just because he's even more witty and gorgeous now doesn't change who he is. I keep the conversation on safe topics and ask Fin about his work.

"I've always enjoyed visual art. Whether it's painting, sketches, photography or moving image, anything really, I love how a simple image, a still of a split second, a moment in someone's life can actually show so much information, depth and feeling." Never breaking eye contact with me, he leans forward and continues, "If our eyes are the windows to our souls, then a photograph taken at the exact, precise, perfect moment, allows that soul to be preserved forever."

"That's a pretty noble reason to be sneaking pictures of people. How do you translate that into taking photographs for the paper?"

"It's not just pictures for the paper though and it's not just pictures of people. For example, at the minute my main goal is to illustrate to the world how beautiful and cultural Northern Ireland is. That's not about taking pictures of people, that's about finding that moment when the sun breaks through the cloud, streaking the countryside below in hues of gold highlighting the different shades of fields and farmlands below. Doesn't that sound like somewhere you would like to visit and see?" It's ridiculous that I'm happy for him. Fin always enjoyed taking photographs, even though it pissed him off I would never let him take my picture. He's managed to get a job doing what he truly loves.

"God, I see that every day, well, when it's not raining, and I've never thought of it like that. I've been too busy focusing on the traffic behind the tractor and the smell of manure from the farms."

"But that's the joy of photography, it can make you sit back and realise the beauty that's been staring you in the face your entire life." He squeezes my thigh and gives me a look that might suggest he's talking about more than the 40 shades of green that can be found in our fields.

The conversation moves on to more banal subjects and we only stop when our next dishes are brought out and we continue eating. Fin continues to drive me crazy, eating with one hand and slowly moving his fingers up and down my thigh; ensuring that the fire he's started in me is continuously stoked.

We finish up our dinner and as Fin excuses himself to go to the bathroom, I finish off my third glass of wine. I don't have much of a chance to assess my situation as Fin places both hands on my shoulders, his thumbs rubbing against the outside of my neck. I can feel the light scratch of the stubble that's forming when he leans downs and whispers in my ear, "Are you ready to get out of here?"

I manage a simple "Mm hm." Honestly, this man manages to scramble my brain cells, even more so with a few glasses of wine. He has my coat lifted and waiting to be placed on me and takes me by the hand once again as he leads me out of the restaurant and towards the car.

The car journey back to my house is different this time because his hand continues to move up and down my thigh. Every so often he extends his little finger so that it strokes me through the seam of my jeans. I can't control the urge to lean back in my seat, not only giving him better access, but me, the perfect view of his profile while he concentrates on driving. I desperately need some relief and soon. When we pull up to my house I have no choice but ask him to come in with me. Whether it's the fact that I'm so turned on I could explode if the wind blows the right way, the wine, or the way Fin has made me not think for one second tonight about what I'm eating, how much I'm eating or what I'll have to do tomorrow to make up for my calorific evening. I can't think of any other way I want to spend tonight than wrapped around Fin.

"Are you sure, Livvy?" He looks lost between wanting to make sure I want this and doing a dance to the Gods to make sure I mean what I said.

It's my turn to take him by the hand and squeeze as I say, "I'm absolutely positive that if you don't come in here tonight with me and make me come, I'm just going to be thinking about you when I go in there and get myself off." He barely has his car door open before he's out and making his way round to my side.

Always the gentleman, even when I can feel his erection pressing into my back, he reaches around to open my front door and hold it open for me. He's directly behind me, hands on my waist, turning me as he kicks the door closed. His lips connect with mine and I immediately sigh at the warmth. Never one to miss an opportunity, Fin delves his tongue into my mouth, somehow managing to make me feel ravaged and cherished at the same time. My back connects with the wall, but he's already moved one hand to the back of my head to protect me from the exposed brick. *Jesus, things like this remind me of the old Fin, my Fin.* He brings both his hands back down to my waist and I'm thankful I wore my sculpting jeans, their support manages to smooth out the lumps and bumps that are hiding there. I must have stiffened or given myself away because he pulls back resting his forehead against mine and looks me in the eye. "Shhh, it's okay. You're beautiful. I love these curves." He accentuates his point by squeezing my hips, making me want to believe him. "I love a woman who actually looks like a woman. Not one that could give me a papercut if I hold her too tight."

His mouth descends to my neck as his hands move underneath my tunic. I don't have any time to worry though as he quickly slides his thumbs along the underside of my breasts, causing my breath to catch in my throat. While stealing all my thoughts in a deep kiss, one hand moves up to squeeze my breast and graze my nipple. His other hand moves down to my jeans, but before he does anything more he leans back, looking me in the eyes while he pinches my nipples, raising an eyebrow in silent question. The nipple pinch brings a porn star moan out of my mouth and I nod at him hopefully conveying just how pissed I'll be if he works me up this much and then doesn't attempt to finish the job.

He gives me a glorious grin that makes me realise that his smirk isn't the biggest weapon in his arsenal and flips open the button of my jeans. I use this opportunity to see if Fin has managed to fill out in every facet of his body in the last decade and run my palm down the front of his jeans. *Jesus Christ, he's gonna split me in two with that thing!* I grab a hold of his cock and start slowly rubbing from tip to base, increasing the pace as the speed of his ministrations on my nipple and zipper increase.

Somehow defying the laws of physics he gets my skinny jeans down to my knees and plunders my mouth one more time while showing my nipple some final love. He slowly moves down to his knees leaving kisses on my breasts and stomach. When he comes face to face with my tight, black spanx he stops cold. "What the…" He looks up at me and smiles. "You're definitely not making this easy for me," he grunts slightly as he manages to grab a hold. He tries to move them but they don't budge. Getting a better grip of the modern day chastity belt he fights with them until they meet the jeans at my knees. He places a kiss on each thigh, thankfully resuming our regularly scheduled programming, undeterred by devil's underwear.

My eyes follow him down and it is a gloriously beautiful view. He peels (*literally* peels because they're *that* tight) my jeans and spanx down and I slip my shoes off one by one as he tugs the offending clothing off each foot with a snap.

His hands slowly caress my calves, his thumb adding a delicious bite of pressure along the way. His eyes are much slower moving as they take in every inch of skin on my legs and eventually my pussy.

"You are so beautiful, Livvy." He casts his eyes up to me and punctuates his sentence by running his thumbs up the inside of my thighs to my centre. And that's it. That's all the warning I get before he uses his thumbs to open me and widen my legs and run his tongue along my slit. His tongue lashes my clit in wide strokes while he uses his thumb to slowly enter and run back and forth along my centre.

He groans into my pussy and hoists one of my legs over his shoulder, opening me up in front of him. His tongue pierces me as he laps at my wetness while his thumb circles my clit adding more and more pressure. I can feel the heat and pressure building in my stomach and slowly but surely moving lower. My fingers grab a hold on his hair because he better not stop what he's doing.

As my grip on his hair increases Fin starts flicking my clit with just the tip of this tongue, going faster and faster as he pushes one finger inside me and hooks it so that he's rubbing against my G-spot. The tornado of pressure inside me just ramped up and I swear I'm about to start hearing angels sing. Adding a second finger and sucking on my clit has my back arching off the wall and my toes curling as I come with so much force I can feel myself gripping his fingers with the walls of my pussy. He alternates back to gently licking my clit and slowly circling his tongue. Just as I start to come down from the high he redoubles his efforts sucking on my clit and rubbing both fingertips against my G-spot. His five o'clock stubble adds a delicious friction and as a second orgasm barrels through me, half the street must be able to hear the guttural groan of satisfaction and Fin's name exclaimed from my lips.

With one last kiss he rises up and takes my mouth in a searing kiss. When he breaks the kiss I can't stop the giggle that erupts. He takes me by the hand and pulls me away from the wall and starts up the stairs. As we pass the first door he glances back at me with a smile on his face and I shake my head, he repeats the process at the second door and nearly takes it off its hinges when I nod that it is my bedroom.

We spin into the room and my hands immediately go to his hair as we start kissing again, our tongues battling and teeth nipping at each other's lips. I can feel his hard cock pressing against me, begging for my attention and I am more than happy to oblige. Putting my hands on his shoulders I push him backwards towards my bed and he sits down. I kneel in front of him and run my hands up his thighs, rubbing my thumbs up either side of his steel shaft. I flick open the first button of his fly and then the second, I'm two more buttons away from the promised land when he starts vibrating.

I give his crotch a confused look as it then starts playing *The Devil Went Down to Georgia*. "Ffuuuccckkkk!" Fin slides back on the bed and reaches into his pocket and pulls out his phone. "I'm so sorry, Livvy," he says, looking down at his dick pressing against the last two buttons, "You have no idea how sorry I am, but I *have* to take this."

Sitting back on my heels I have literally no words right now. Who stops getting a blowjob, or at least what was the start of getting a blowjob to take a fucking phone call? Given that I can only hear Fin's side of the conversation I have not a fucking clue what is happening right now. He simply answers with one-word replies or grunts and finishes the conversation with a, "Right, I'm on my way."

Running his hand down his face I can tell from the conversation and the look he's currently giving me that this is not going to end well for me. I want to be able to ask what's going on, I want to be able to demand that he doesn't walk out on me right now while I'm literally on my knees in front of him. But I can't seem to speak around the lump that's blocking my throat.

Fin stands up and redoes his fly. He takes my face in his hand and rubs his thumb across my cheekbone and kisses me on the forehead. "I'm so sorry, but I *really* have to go." He at least has the decency to look sheepish as he walks out of my bedroom. The sound of my front door slamming shut is the only thing that interrupts the sound of my quiet sobs.

Chapter Seven

'To have a good enemy, choose a friend, he knows where to strike.'
- Diane de Poitiers

I'm walking down the corridor to my History class. The corridors are lined with pupils all watching me. I had to go to the bathroom so I couldn't get to class first and avoid running this gauntlet. I try to pick up the pace of my steps but I'm called up short when someone shouts, "slow down Bessie, it feels like an earthquake." This is quickly followed up by someone else calling out, "watch out! Make room! Elephant coming through!" I don't need to look up to know it's Fiona and Sinead with their usual barbs. They've already alienated me from everyone else. Any poor unfortunate soul who tried to make friends with me, met the same fate as me, and really, there's only so much a person can put up with before they realise I'm not worth the daily battle.

I break my own rule and give them my attention when I hear from behind me, "fuck off, Fiona, isn't there somebody you should be sucking off about now?" I manage a small relieved smile as Fin comes up behind me and puts his arm across my shoulder, shielding me physically and emotionally. I feel some of the tension leave me and I keep pace with him.

"Oh that's right, I forgot. You can't go anywhere without your beard, can you, Fin Kelly?" It's not the worst abuse I've heard Fiona shout and really, coming from her small, slender body and heart-shaped face it destroys any physical beauty she has, but no one else here can see past the outside. They're all like little Stepford Bitches, following her around and trying to look and act like her. If I wasn't subjected to this multiple times a day, I might actually feel sorry for her.

Fin spins us both around and he simply states, "speaking of beards, you might want to go check yours out, I think your bleach missed a spot." Fiona just lets out an indolent screech and takes off towards the bathroom followed by her minions.

"Come on, Elizabeth, let's get to class." So we walk down the corridor in blissful silence, with no one making eye contact with either of us, Fin's warm arm slung across my shoulder wrapping me in his musky scent and protecting me in every way that counts.

Suddenly the corridor darkens and I find myself sitting on my bed in my room completely alone, crying. I can't believe he didn't show up. I can't believe after he convinced me to go to the school formal and my mum and dad saved up to get me a dress, he didn't show up. After the first 30 minutes I started to worry, I knew something was wrong. When he was 45 minutes late I phoned his house in case something had had happened on his way here. I could feel my blood run cold when his mother answered, her speech more slurry than normal when she barked, "what?" down the phone at me.

"Sorry, Mrs. Kelly, is Fin there? Has he left yet?"

Laughing down the line at me she answers, "no, he's not here, he's away to his party. You didn't really think he was going to take you, Elizabeth, did you? My boy has much better and less bigger things waiting for him." She keeps cackling down the phone at me, then spits out, "silly, stupid, Bessie, that's what the kids call you isn't it? 'Bessie the Elephant'? Well, Bessie, my Fin finally saw the light and he won't be coming to you anymore." I barely hear the ring tone after she hangs up over the sound of my crying as I rush upstairs and lock myself in my bedroom.

As I spend the night crying in my room, without the energy to even take off my dress, I make a decision. I'm not letting any of them win. I don't know what I did to turn Fin and I don't think I'll forget or forgive him for this. We had talked and planned, we were going to give each other our virginities tonight. I don't know what's happening right now or what I've done to deserve this. But I know that without him walking beside me in school I'm not going to last much longer. My last exam is in a week, once I finish it I'm not stepping foot back in that school. I'm going to transfer out and do my last two years somewhere else.

If he wants to cut me off I'll take that hurt. But I'm going to use it. I'll protect myself this next week, use every plan and trick I've ever had to use before so they won't get me alone for a single second and then when I'm gone I'll never have to see a single one of them again.

I lie here crying for everything that's happened, everything I've lost and everything I will still have to go through; I just hope that having a plan to follow will make the ache spreading through my body with each beat of my heart, hurt a little less.

I wake with a start at my alarm and run my hand down my face, not particularly surprised when it comes away wet. I knew this was going to happen. It was a risk getting close to Fin again that the nightmares and flashbacks would come back. I can see two nights of it in a row have taken their toll when I look in the mirror. The 36 hours of studiously avoiding and ignoring Fin's calls and texts haven't helped matters either. I can't think of a single good reason for walking out on me, especially when he knew it was my first time in two years. He wound up the spring and then didn't give it the release it needed.

I get myself ready and out the door for a full day's teaching. Concealer and coffee are my friends today so I don't look like the walking dead. I get into my office and start my computer running while I take a look at my planner for the day. I've two double-session lectures with an hour of student consultations in between. I'm not sure there's enough coffee beans in Columbia to keep me going today.

My first lecture is two hours extolling the virtues of Irish literature. It's a new short course which a lot of students have picked up for extra credit or as part of a professional development course. It usually means that a lot of questions aren't asked until we start having the smaller seminar groups and dissecting the different texts.

I call into the on-campus coffee shop and get a venti, which will hopefully get me through this first lecture. The great thing is Irish Literature is one of my great loves, so getting to talk for two hours about Oscar Wilde and WB Yeats isn't really hardship. Once I have my slideshow set up I take a quick look at the auditorium. There's more students than I'd been expecting but I find the best way to do this and not get stage fright, is to never focus in past the first row. If I'm not looking at them, I'm looking at the windows along the back of the wall, slightly higher than the heads of the 'cool kids' sitting in the back row.

I notice Silent Bob in the front row and quickly mask my shock. It shouldn't surprise me that he's here, even when he is high, his work is exceptional. I probably should have rethought my lesson plan for this lecture as we're beginning with *The Importance of Being Earnest* focusing on the deception throughout the play and the fact that Wilde imitates life through art. At least I can now say I understand part of the thinking behind these characters and their need for deceit.

By the time my two hours are up I've been so in the zone that I was able to forget what a complete and utter fool I made of myself on Saturday night. I still can't believe he just walked out. Who could've possibly been on the other end of that phone call? Oh God, what if he already has a girlfriend? I wouldn't put it past him, anyone that could turn on me like he did could easily deceive a girlfriend, or worse, a wife.

I barely even register Silent Bob holding the door open for me but manage to glance a smile his way and I'm thankful that I must be keeping my game face on well because he smiles back at me, which for Bob, is quite a feat. I make a mental note to actually check what his real name is in case he ever musters the nerve to actually speak a full sentence to me.

I make a beeline for the coffee shop for some more liquid fuel before I head to my office and meet with any students who've made an appointment or just land at my door. My phone vibrating grabs my attention and I get just a second to read the message from Mark that said, *I'm sorry*, before I walk into a wall. Except it's not a wall because walls don't smell this good and I'm sure I'll remember this smell until the day I die. I look up and see the one person I've been actively avoiding thinking about for the past day and a half.

"How did you know where to find me?" I know my voice sounds harsh, I want it to sound harsh, I'm pissed way the fuck off after how he left things on Saturday night. He rightly looks contrite and quickly glances around.

"Do you have a few minutes to talk?" he asks and takes my hand.

A snatch my hand out of his and repeat, "How did you know where to find me?" He either doesn't read social cues or he's feeling homicidal because he takes my hand again and starts walking me towards an empty table that is thankfully at the coffee shop.

"Mark told me where to find you. I explained to him what happened and after he threatened to gouge my balls out with a rusty spoon he told me what your schedule was and where I was likely to find you."

"So, you're actively choosing to keep me away from caffeine. You are aware that Mark's not the only one who'll gouge your damn balls out, right?" He's still holding my hand and apparently I acted too quickly before because every time I go to yank it away he holds on that little bit tighter.

Stroking his thumb across my wrist, seriously he must know what that move does to me and he's pulling out all the stops, he begs, "Just give me five minutes, Livvy, five minutes and then I'll let you go." I don't know what I want to say right now so I just give him a short nod, so he continues on. "There's some things about me I haven't told you yet. I just, I just don't really like to talk about it. It's not something that comes up in normal conversation."

"So help me God if you tell me you have a wife or a girlfriend at home, I don't give a shit if it's an open relationship I will walk away right the fuck now, Fin."

He starts sounding confused and quickly moves on to amused as he continues, "No, no, no, no girlfriend and definitely no wife. I just have a lot of things going on in the background at the minute. Part of which is why I've moved back up North. I'm asking you to trust me, to just wait a little while and I'll tell you absolutely everything."

He looks so incredibly sincere and as if possible it makes him look even more attractive, there's no walls around him right now. He's letting me see all of him at this moment I realise that I'm being a hell of hypocrite if I hold it against him that he doesn't want to keep something to himself considering how many secrets I'm keeping from him.

"I can't guarantee that won't happen again, but I'm working on making it a lot less likely, I promise." He takes my other hand as he speaks to me and squeezes both hands gently, willing me to listen to him, to believe him.

"Okay, I can understand you wanting to keep some things to yourself, I mean, we're not even really a 'we' so I can't really hold you to anything, except of course, basic manners."

"What do you mean not really a 'we'? I don't know about you, Lizzy, but when I spend a good portion of my night with my face between a woman's thighs I consider myself to be part of a 'we'."

I can't really refute that, so I don't. "Yes, well, I didn't want to make an assumption. Not all men feel the same way."

"Have you not realised by now, Livvy? I'm nothing like all men." He states as if it were an irrefutable fact like the earth is round or you can't lick your own elbow. "So we've established that we are in fact a 'we' and there's one other thing you need to know. I don't share, so this is the only 'we' you're going be a part of, yes."

Even though it's not a question, I feel like he's waiting for an answer. "Yeah, I don't share either so it goes both ways, Fin."

"Well, hopefully this will help me get back into your good graces then. As part of my assignment I have to experience the nightlife and attractions the paper is focussing on. They're hoping that by identifying and obviously photographing everything Northern Ireland can provide, especially through the eyes of a prodigal son, the tourist board and some of the national papers might pick it up too. So, I basically get to go out and visit some of this country's most famous restaurants, museums and locales and I really don't want to do that alone." He leans across the table, still holding my hands, never breaking the connection between us, "Would you like to come with me and experience the very finest that Northern Ireland has to offer?"

Well, there was only one answer I could give to that really, wasn't there?

Chapter Eight

'Nobody speaks the truth when there's something they must have.'
-Elizabeth Bowen

The rest of week passes, thankfully, uneventfully. Though every night, Fin and I text or call each other. Nothing huge, nothing substantial, just idle conversation passing the time. Where he went today, who he got to interview and picture. What classes I had, who had the best excuse for not having their assignment finished. That excuse went to Clare, who claims that in a fever-induced delirium, she tried to use her fireplace to get to Diagon Alley and gave herself a concussion.

Thai Tuesday went ahead as normal, it's an extra perk from having your best friend live two houses down and a Thai restaurant at the end of the street. Technically, Mark's closer so he always goes to pick it up, but we always eat in my house because it's cleaner. Given that I barely tidy up once a month, that should give you an idea of how messy Mark actually is.

Mark made sure he was given every detail possible about Saturday night. The fact that Mark and I aren't remotely attracted to each other means these conversations are actually a learning opportunity. Believe me when I say the best blow job advice you can get is from a man. Although he does keep threatening to name and patent his moves.

I also got an apology from him for telling Fin where to find me but apparently it was, 'impossible to resist his puppy dog eyes,' I swear I don't care if they're gay, straight or bi, men can't resist a pretty face that bats their eyelashes.

There's no match this weekend so Mark plans on going out Friday night and trying to improve upon last week's score. I had to face telling him that my plans consisted of vegging out and reading all weekend. Even though Fin was quick to ask me to go out with him again, he hasn't mentioned it once all week.

By the time Friday rolls around and I'm only on a half day teaching, I've resigned myself to doing sweet fuck all this weekend. In fairness, it's probably best to appreciate not having to get up at the ass crack of dawn for a rugby match on the Saturday and then the inevitable hangover on the Sunday. *Hmm a hangover-free Sunday, what are those?*

My thoughts and progress in to work are interrupted by a text from Fin.

7pm tonight. Your house. Dress warm.

Christ it's annoying how hot it is when he bosses me around. I spend the rest of my commute going over what I could wear that's both sexy and warm and where we could be going that requires me to dress warm. It's October so I know it's going to have to be somewhere outside but that doesn't exactly narrow it down.

Settling in behind my desk, I'm stopped from my mind wandering further by my phone.

"Hi, Mum, what's up?" I obviously haven't mentioned Fin to my mum because, a) eww we're close but not *that* close; and b) she was both devastated and enraged by what happened with Fin before, so I really don't want to court a lecture right now.

"Nothing's up, sweetheart. I just wanted to phone and see how you are. Are you planning on coming home soon?" Her sweetness doesn't fool me. I know she's up to something, but knowing my mum, God only knows what.

"Mmm hmm, I believe you. Thousands wouldn't, but I do."

"Oh you shush now. I just wanted to know if you were going to come home for your school reunion."

"What school reunion, Mum?"

"St Ignacious, silly. They're doing their school reunion early this year. Geraldine in the hairdressers was telling me. You know, I know you didn't have a good time there baby girl, but maybe this is the perfect chance to throw it in their faces. I mean, you're a published academic, you're a lecturer at a prestigious university..."

"And I'm half the size I used to be," I interrupt, already exasperated.

"Don't you dare, Elizabeth Virginia McKeen!" she snaps, "You know I don't give a single damn about what you weigh. But you are a successful, self-confident young woman and you deserve the opportunity to rub those bitches' noses in it." I love my mum. I think she would rip apart anyone who did wrong by me with her bare hands.

"I know, Mum, really, I do," *and maybe if I say it often enough I'll believe it more,* "I'll think about it, okay? Why are they inviting me anyway? I left two years before anyone else."

"I don't know, sweetheart, I'm assuming they're inviting everyone who left at sixteen and eighteen." There's a suspicious pause before she speaks again, "So, you're not going to be coming home soon then?" She's a persistent woman when there's something she wants.

"Depending on when this school reunion is, no, I'm not." I manage to avoid sighing, just.

"I've got some post for you here. None of it seems particularly urgent so I'll wait until there's a bit of a pile and then forward it all on to you, honey." She tries to not sound too sad, but she doesn't mask it as well as she hopes. It's difficult for me going home. To most people home is a place of refuge, your last stand against the brutality of life. My memories of home are stained with tears, heartbreak and a feeling that life would never get any better. My family did their best to raise me up on their shoulders, to help elevate me above the smog of depression that surrounded me. But until I was removed from the situation I was mired in in school, their efforts fruitless.

"Thanks, Mum, I promise I'll try and come home before Christmas." I do mean it, but life has a way of slipping through your fingers and before you know it, days become weeks, which become months in the blink of an eye. "Mum, I've literally just sat down at work, do you mind if I phone you back later?"

"Not a problem, honey, I'll talk to you later, God bless." She ends every single phone call this way, could be me, the pope or a freaking telemarketer but she'll pass on her hope that the big man upstairs watches over them.

"God bless, Mum, love you."

Now I have to try to multitask getting ready for my lecture and wardrobe planning.

• • •

Trying to dress warm and sexy is not an easy feat. I've decided to go for a few light layers rather than one big bulky jumper. Still warm but when adjusted the right way, puts my legs and the girls on display. Since I've dressed warmly it's too hot to wait about in my house so I lock up and make my way down to the front gate. The sky is perfectly clear, an immeasurable cloth of stars emphasising the complete lack of clouds.

Fin's car pulls up and he leaves the engine running as he hops out and comes over to me. He catches me before I can open the door and spins me around against the car. Opening my mouth to rebuke him for manhandling me I'm caught off guard when he kisses me so fiercely I have to lean back against the car to stay upright while I wrap my arms around his neck.

He pushes the knit cap off my head and pulls my hair until I feel the slight sting and move my head giving him free access to my neck. He works down past my ear to my jaw line, meandering, taking his time and relishing in the way I grip his shoulders, digging in my fingertips. When he reaches where the muscle in my neck meets my shoulder he gently bites down and then slowly moves back. The hands that had been around my back slowly trace down each rib as he moves his hands to my hips, steadying me. If he wasn't holding on to me right now there's a very real chance I would be a puddle of oestrogen at his feet.

"I've been jonesing all week to get to do that." He finishes by giving me another short kiss. *Words, people reply with words right about now.*

"Hi," *Brain, you have a 140 IQ, I need you to do your damn job.*

He must think my brain fart's cute because he smiles, "Hi yourself," and steps back.

Now I get to take in and appreciate the specimen before me. Dressed in a black leather jacket over a slate coloured thermal top, topped off with dark blue denim jeans and black converse, he's quite a feast for the eyes. "Come on, let's go get you fed, if you keep looking at me like that the only place we'll be going is back into your apartment."

Not that I have any arguments with that plan. He reaches around me to open my door and makes his way round to the driver's side. He has to adjust himself twice before he gets into the car so at least I'm not the only one worked up after that little hello.

43

My eyes are glued to the countryside that's whizzing by me as we drive down the winding road that's nothing but short brick wall and then still, black sea on one side and quick changing landscape on the other. Every few miles the scenery changes from cliff faces, to masses of green fields bleached of all colour in the moonlight to villages full of white and terracotta coloured houses.

Just as we enter into the village of Glenarm, the marina full of small fishing boats and houses of all shapes and sizes, we turn left and start driving up a steep road sweeping around the base of the hills that frame the village.

We keep climbing higher, driving past the castle and it's gardens which stretch on for miles. Once we've reached the apex of the hill, Fin pulls into a gravel lay-by which points the windscreen back towards the way we came. The view from this position is breathtaking. Where we sit, the valley that nature carved into the earth re-joins the elevation and we can see right down miles of countryside to where the twinkling lights of the marina meet the sea. It's dark enough now that only the moon casts any light, save the small reflected sliver from the lighthouse that casts shadows on the small swelling waters.

I've been so engrossed in the nature that lies before me that I haven't even noticed Fin get out of the car and come around to my door; until he takes me by the hand and simply says, "Come."

We walk around the side of the car and Fin produces a picnic basket and a camera case. "I'm sorry, but part of this will have to be a working dinner, I'm afraid." Bumping the door shut with his hip, he leads us to a space in the short boundary wall. Not letting go of my hand he helps me over the rocky terrain until we reach a clearing in the field just before the slope begins.

Laying out a blanket, Fin sits me down and rummages through the picnic basket. He produces a couple of plastic plates and Tupperware boxes. Popping each box open I can see and smell a mixture of aromas. The warm yeast of fresh baguette, the nutty tang of camembert and the herbs and spices from different cooked meats. I can feel myself smile as I realise he's managed to pack an entire meat platter into the picnic basket.

"I know it's not a three-course meal but I thought it would be nice if we ate alfresco tonight." He shrugs as if he doesn't realise just how sweet he's being.

"No, it's perfect Fin, thank you." He gives me a slight nod and reaches into the basket once more. He sits back on his heels with two plastic long-stemmed glasses in one hand and bottle of sparkling cider. He must have chilled it before we left because I can see the condensation running over the lip of the label.

"Trust me when I say you'll want to experience tonight with a clear head." Popping the cork off the glass bottle he pours us both a glass and passes me a plate and cutlery.

"So what is it we're here to photograph?" Popping a piece of chicken in my mouth, I lean back on my elbows and let the countryside settle around me.

"Not telling just yet, Livvy. Enjoy your dinner and the scenery, you'll get to see why we're here soon enough." We both roll onto our sides with our plates in front of us. It's strangely intimate eating whilst lying facing someone. No such thing as avoiding eye contact. Any lapses into silence aren't uncomfortable. We both just listen to the wildlife or rumbling of a stream that must run nearby down to the sea. "What area of literature is it ya teach then?"

"Mostly Elizabethan and Irish literature."

"Does that mean ya only read about madmen running about and shouting in the moors?"

I narrowly avoid snorting cider out my nose. "No, there's only so much old school literature I can take in a day. I'll read anything you put in front of me. I'm not saying I'll enjoy it, but I'll give anything a go at least once."

"Yeah, I get that. I enjoy taking photographs and displaying emotion through it, but I'm not gonna spend all my free time dissecting every picture I see. But what was it that lured you to literature?"

"Well, it's the same reason why I could understand your reasoning for photography last week. Good writing tells you just as much about the author as the subject matter. A writer puts their life, heart and soul into their writing and can use it to invoke passion, empathy and understanding when it's put into the right readers' hands."

"So, in our own ways we're both creative souls, I suppose." Fin leans across the remains of the dinner strewn around the blanket to give me a short, deep kiss. "Lie back and take in the view while I clear up these dishes."

Not one for arguing, at least when it means I get to relax, I do as he tells me and lie back on the blanket so I can gaze up at the night sky. Being so high up and so removed from civilization means there's no light pollution and I can see every visible star, planet and whizzing satellite.

I must get lost in the view because the whizz of a camera shutter snaps my attention back to Earth and I notice that all the dishes, bar our drinks, have been tidied away and Fin is currently pointing his camera at me. I quickly try to cover my face, "What are you doing? Stop that."

He just laughs and keeps taking my picture while trying and unfortunately succeeding in prying my fingers away from my face. The fluttering in my stomach is surreal. The genuine happiness from this moment is something I didn't believe I'd get to experience again. Certainly not with Fin Kelly, of all people. The emotion catches me off guard. I'm not given any time to process it because Fin laces his fingers with mine, looking up at the sky he simply says, "Watch."

As we lie there the sky slowly starts to light up as if sheets of rain were falling. Tracks of green light, whisper thin but so immense they light the whole sky slowly begin to turn purple and red followed by differing hues of green. Wave after wave of light enter our line of sight, traversing their way across the sky. Their every movement tracked by the trail of celestial light left behind them. I don't even realise that I've gripped onto Fin's hand in awe until he has to release it to adjust his camera settings. He's been snapping pictures this whole time.

I have no idea how long has passed when I register the silence. Fin's stopped taking photos and is just watching the incredible light show with me. The vulnerability of this moment is the wakeup call I need. I can't forget who I am and how far I've come. This Fin might be sweet and gentle but I know what lies underneath. I need to remember why I'm here.

I grab his attention by squeezing his fingers and he looks over at me with what appears to be pure joy; but I know better. I make my way over to him on my hands and knees, hoping the extra wiggle I put in my ass makes this move seductive and not like I'm trying to dislodge a wedgie.

I straddle his lap and take his face in my hands, cutting off his view of the sky. Keeping eye contact I lean down, making my intentions clear and close my eyes just as I take his mouth in a vibrant kiss. I pour all my conflicting, irreconcilable emotions into this kiss. His hands immediately grasp my waist and he sits up, resting my full weight on his lap where I can feel he's already hard for me. *For me!* I can't deny the small thrill from knowing that I can make Fintan Kelly hard. If he knew who I really was he would be embarrassed for himself. I'm overjoyed for the 16-year-old me that never thought this day would come.

Fin pulls me down on to his hard length and I'm sure he can feel the heat coming off me, even through my leggings and his denim. As he pulls me down he shifts his hips up so he's rubbing my clit through our clothes. Just as I feel like I'm in control of the kiss and I have him exactly where I want him – under me, he flips us over. His mouth is now the one hot against mine as he nips at my bottom lip and takes my mouth in a kiss that steals the breath from my lungs.

He moves my hands above my head and holds them there as he presses the lower half of his body into mine, grinding his hips against the apex of my thighs. In between kisses he orders me to, "Open," kiss, "your," kiss, "legs." I comply immediately, opening further and am rewarded with the sweet friction of his rock-hard cock against my clit. Restraining both hands with one of his, he works his way down to my ass hitching my leg up on his hip. When I begin to move back against him, he groans down my throat, tightening his grip on my head, silently commanding me to keep it there. With the pressure building in my belly I don't think I could move my leg if I tried.

Fin moves his hand up to my breast, squeezing and rubbing his thumb over my nipple. He unzips my jacket and his hand returns to its previous position but this time with much less fabric hindering its progress. He pulls away and I look up to see why he's stopped. He rests his forehead against mine, panting heavily, "Livvy, I've been dying to have you since last week, so I'm going to ask this once. We are out in the middle of fucking nowhere with nothing but the stars watching us. The minute you say yes I am going to take you right here in this field."

He punctuates his need by grinding into me one more time, "God, yes, now Fin." If he doesn't make me come in the next three seconds I will end up causing him an injury. I've been walking around with blue clit for the past week after his early departure. Even faithful BOB wasn't up to the challenge, or the battery power required.

He wasn't joking when he said my affirmation was all he needed. He kisses me again, redoubling the efforts of his tongue and his cock when I hear him mutter, "Fuck it," and he releases my hands to pull my tunic up past my breasts and pulling each cup down, thrusting their mounds out for his awaiting hands. Taking each breast in a hand he pinches and pulls at my left nipple while he holds the right, ready for his hot mouth. Sucking on the nipple and biting down he quickly salves it with his tongue before changing over, taking my left in his mouth and working my right with his hand. All the while he continuously pumps against me, rocking against me harder and faster. If he keeps up this pace I'm going to come before he even has me naked.

He kisses down my stomach, I notice his eyes quickly glance over the stretch marks from where I put on and lost weight so often, but apart from quickly glancing up to my eyes he makes no comment. Leaning behind him he pulls off my boots and runs his eyes from my pussy up to my face. When my feet are free, he grabs the waist band and pulls my boy shorts down along with my leggings; never losing eye contact with me. "I'm sorry, Livvy, but before we do anything else I need another taste." I lose eye contact with him as he buries his face in my pussy and darts his tongue inside me while he rubs my clit in short, tight circles with his thumb.

He sucks on my clit, laving it with his tongue, ratcheting up the explosion ready to combust. He thrusts two fingers inside me and curls them upwards rubbing them against the small bundle of nerves hidden there – like orgasm nirvana. It's enough to push me over the edge and I clamp down on his fingers, my own shooting straight to his hair to hold him in place. No thoughts of him needing oxygen enter my mind as I chase the pleasure coursing through me. As my convulsions start to wane I loosen my grip on his hair and he pulls back, running his tongue broadly one last time the full length of me. When he emerges from between my legs he has a shit-eating grin on his face and darts forward to kiss me, plunging his tongue into my mouth where I can taste myself all over him.

He sits back and fumbles for his wallet in his back pocket while I make quick work of his fly and delve my hand into his boxers, immediately being greeted by his hot, silky length. I run my thumb over the head feeling the wetness of how turned on he is and use it to ease the glide of my hand down his shaft.

"That's enough of that, Livvy or this is going to be over before it's started." He quickly stands kicking off his shoes and ridding himself of boxers and jeans in one smooth move. He removes the condom from his wallet which he then throws on top of his jeans. The aurora borealis is still shining brightly behind him giving him a magnificent halo. I would have thought there was nothing hotter than a man ripping a condom open between his teeth while he devours you with his eyes. I was wrong. Watching him while he does it back lit with a celestial light show and finally getting to see the glory of the long, hard cock that he strokes up and down just before sheathing himself is infinitesimally better.

He walks over to me and moves down onto his knees, placing his hands at each of my shoulders. "God, Livvy," he exhales whilst he rubs the head of his cock against my clit, two, three times, before sliding down to my opening. He kisses me deeply, thrusting his tongue in my mouth just as he thrusts his cock inside me, causing me to arch and cry out in his mouth.

He continues to kiss me, just keeping his length inside me giving me time to adjust to the intrusion. The fact that it's been two years and his considerable length makes it a snug fit, not painful but secure, perfect. He runs his hand down my side, being sure to rub the hard nub of my nipple with his thumb along the way. He takes my leg, behind the knee, lifting my leg over his hip, running his fingertips down the underside of my leg, taking my ass cheek in his hand as he slides in even further, deeper, I have the overwhelming sensation of being full and hoping that he doesn't have any further left to enter because I'm pretty sure he's close to touching my womb.

He must notice my face relax because he starts moving, slowly at first, pulling out until just the tip remains and just as painstakingly slowly enters me again. He starts to move quicker, rubbing his pubic bone against my clit each time he's fully seated and rubbing the head of his cock against my G-spot each time he pulls back. I start lifting my hips meeting him thrust for thrust, arching my back off the ground. He takes my nipple in his mouth, sucking and nipping with his teeth. His other hand reaches round and splays across my back, keeping me in that position so he can have his fill while he continues to spear me, each thrust against my clit and my G-spot pushing me closer to the knife edge.

Just as Fin pushes into the root, the hand at my back lifts me up and he sits back on his heels, bringing us eye to eye and adding to the pressure on my clit. I start undulating my hips, rocking and rotating, adding delicious friction. As Fin kisses me again, piercing me with his tongue, I start lifting myself up, almost removing myself completely and slamming back down, increasing my speed until we're no longer kissing, just lips touching, panting into each other's mouth, groaning and gasping as we each climb higher. As my thighs start quivering both from exertion and anticipation, Fin takes control, grasping my hips. Lifting me up and plunging me back down we both freefall at the same time, each calling out the other's name.

Softly he places me back down onto the blanket and gently withdraws, kissing my breastbone as he resituates my bra and top. Through some magic, that only men seem to have, he has the condom off and tied in a split second. As much as I would love some post outdoors snuggling, if I don't get dressed soon I'm liable to lose body parts from the cold. Fin must have the same thought because he quickly chases down my clothes from their surrounding spots and brings them over before jumping into his own jeans. Once we're both wrapped up again he takes me by the hand, kissing me once more, and helps me negotiate the field back to the car.

Chapter Nine

'She stood in the storm, and when the wind did not blow her way, she adjusted her sails.'
-Elizabeth Edwards

Fin drops me back at my house with a promise to call me tomorrow to organise our next adventure. But as we make our way up to my door, I notice a light on downstairs that I'm certain I turned off.

"Did you leave that light on?" Fin asks, moving me behind him as we approach the door.

"No, I switched everything off, like normal."

Just as we reach the door, I hear the unmistakable guffaw of Mark's laugh and feel the tension drain from my body as quickly as it entered. "It's just Mark, though I've no idea why he's here, he was supposed to be going out tonight." I move around Fin and go to open the door, my key barely touches the lock when the door is opened from the inside. Fin catches me with his arm around my waist before I fly face first into Mark.

"Livvy! You dirty stop out, where were you?" He looks over my shoulder, "Ahh, there's where you've been."

"Any chance of letting us in, Mark, before bits start freezing and falling off?" Fin asks, prompting Mark to finally stop blocking the doorway and let us through, where I find Josie lounging on the recliner with a glass of wine in her hand and half a bottle left on the table beside Mark's glass. There's the detritus of a night of movies and gorging on fast food spread all over my living room. It's like a comfort-food graveyard in here.

"While I appreciate the welcoming home party, why exactly are the two of you in my house?"

They answer showing absolutely no remorse for using my emergency key and setting up in my house while I'm not there. "You said you weren't doing anything tonight," Mark starts.

"So, we decided to call round and keep you company," Josie finishes their bizarre sentence that neither of them seem to realise doesn't actually answer my question. Tilting my head to the side and raising my eyebrows they thankfully explain their continuing presence in my house.

"You have an open fireplace and a better TV than we do," Mark unashamedly admits while he sinks into my plush chair, skilfully not spilling any of the red wine out of the goblet.

Turning towards Fin he holds me by my waist and pulls me so close that I rest my hands on his shoulders. I fight the need to grope the muscles in his shoulders and arms and focus on his face, his perfectly tousled hair, his twinkling green eyes which seem almost iridescent in this light and his smirk which tells me that...crap I got lost looking at him and he's noticed. Shaking my head both at myself and to clear my thoughts, "I swear it's not as stalkerish as it sounds. I do have a pretty kick ass TV, and for reasons that I'm now doubting, I gave them both a key."

"So, I'm thinking that I can just get up extra early tomorrow and head back to my place then," Fin states as he pulls me even closer. I move my hands up into his hair – I have to seriously focus on our conversation and not the fact that I'm running my fingers through his hair like I'm checking out the symmetry of his cut.

When his words seep in, I can't and don't want to hide the smile that breaks out, "Maybe I can think of a good way to wake you up early, you know to make it worth your while."

"Olivia, tonight's already been more than worth my while. But if I stay, I promise I'll be making it worth yours at least twice more." *Be still my beating clit.*

Before my ovaries have the chance to jump out of my throat, hold on to him and never let go, there's a bout of unrealistic coughing and the sound of two people who are getting uncomfortable with the sexual tension that's amping up in the room.

Mark continues coughing, "Sorry must be all the pheromones in the room," more ridiculous coughing, "Josie, fancy heading out and finishing our movie marathon at my place?" Clearly not even waiting for her answer Mark starts packing up both of their things, of course leaving the mess for me to clean up.

"Sounds good to me. I will say, I'm loving you living so close to Livvy, especially when it's cold as balls outside." Josie at least attempts to move their mess into one manageable pile before joining Mark on his quick escape.

Wrapping themselves up in hats and coats as if they were making an arduous journey to the North Pole and not three doors down, they make their way out the door, Mark walking backwards with a lascivious grin, "Have fun you two."

I don't even wait until they've hit the bottom step before I have my door closed and Fin has me pinned up against it. His hands move straight to my hair, tugging, positioning my head where he wants it, exposing the column of my neck where he immediately zones in kissing, licking and gently biting his way down. Before he gets any further we push away from the door. I take him by the hand and lead him to my room; where he makes good on his promise.

• • •

I wake up the next morning, far too warm for the middle of October. Before my mind starts going overboard and trying to work out if I've perhaps started going through menopause at the age of 28 and currently experiencing a hot flash, my pillow starts flexing and moving. The events from last night break through the morning fog in a succession of increasingly satisfying flashes.

Between the heat of Fin's body and the heat of my memories I instinctively rub my ass against Fin's morning wood which is getting even harder. "Morning sweetness," Fin greets me, placing his hand on my stomach; his fingers grazing my pubic bone, and using his hand to pull me back fully against his waiting erection. I'm enjoying the heat and the feeling of being surrounded by Fin so much that I barely flinch when his hand connects with the softer part of my stomach. I wonder if he either feels the flinch or is simply more aware than I'd given him credit for, but he strokes my stomach in a soothing motion with his thumb as he begins to nuzzle into my neck, using the arm my head is resting on to bring me closer to him.

"What time is your interview today?" I manage to ask in between panting breaths.

"Well, you managed to sleep through me getting a phone call earlier where he phoned to cancel. Something about being short staffed in the restaurant so he was having to work rather than answer my questions. We rescheduled for later in the week."

"Excellent, yay for the hungover waitstaff all over the world calling in sick." I finish with a moan as Fin slides his hand lower and starts tracing my pussy with his fingertips.

"You know what this means, don't you? I get to take my sweet time with you."

Just as Fin's hand starts to work up some friction and he brings his other hand down to my breast we're interrupted by the sound of metal bouncing off the floor and muffled curses from downstairs. I sit up and reach for my spare glasses on my nightstand, grabbing the first piece of clothing I put my hand to, so I can see what the hell is going on in my kitchen.

As luck would have it I've grabbed Fin's thermal from the night before and even luckier, because Fin's a lot taller and more muscled than I am, it's a bit big on me and actually covers my ass. My glasses are next because otherwise I'm more likely to walk into the door rather than through it. Before I can put my hand on the handle Fin's arm bands around me and pulls me back.

Looking at me like I've grown a second nose, Fin whisper shouts, "Are you crazy?"

"What?"

"You hear a noise downstairs and you're going to go down looking like that, when you have no idea who's there!" I'm sure he meant it as a question but it comes out more like an angry statement.

"Fin, I'm pretty sure it's going to be either Mark or Josie; they both have a key and I'm sure a burglar wouldn't be going through my pots and pans in my kitchen."

"You don't know!"

"Really, Fin?" I can see him trying to hold on to his anger but it's a losing battle.

"How do you know it's Mark or Josie, and how do you know they're in your kitchen?"

"The kitchen is directly underneath us and Mark fucks up my pots every time he tries to take the frying pan out of the cupboard. It's not a stretch."

"Fine, it *might* be Mark but I'm still going down first, just in case."

"Okay," I stretch the word out as I open the door for him to walk past.

We make our way to the kitchen where I'm proved right. Josie and Mark are trying to quietly bicker over a pan of eggs.

"I told you, you woke them up!"

"Shut up Josie, you weren't exactly quiet on your feet either!"

"Guys, while I appreciate that you're in my home unannounced once again, why are you here?"

"Well, we felt bad about interrupting your night last night so we thought we'd make you breakfast as an apology." Mark shrugs as if it were the most normal statement to ever make. "But we didn't realise you weren't alone."

"Fin's interview got postponed so he decided to stay later and you've interrupted what was going to be a very happy morning."

"So those better be some amazing eggs," adds Fin.

"Shit, I'm sorry man, there's nothing worse than a cock block. We'll put on extra bacon. Nice abs by the way."

"And on that note, Fin and I are going upstairs to get dressed."

We barely get the door closed when Fin takes my breath in a scorching kiss. "What was that for?"

"Nothing, you just look extra hot in those glasses. Black rims suit you."

"They're just my spares in case I run out of contacts."

"You should wear them more often; they look good on you."

"Maybe. I've kinda got used to my contacts now. We should really get dressed, I wouldn't be surprised if one of them ended up finding an excuse to come up here and ogle your abs a bit more." Reaching up on my tiptoes I give him an equally scorching kiss back

Once we're both, unfortunately, fully dressed, we head back downstairs, thankfully not to the smell of burning food. I'm holding out hope they haven't fucked up breakfast because I am starving and it ain't pretty when I'm hangry. It's becoming apparent just how bad Mark and Josie must be feeling to have interrupted my sexy times twice when we walk into the kitchen to fresh orange juice, scrambled eggs, toast, mountains of bacon and a fresh cafetiere of coffee. It smells like heaven itself. I don't function well without caffeine in the morning so this will definitely make me less likely to hulk up and kill someone.

"Wow guys, you must be feeling really shitty, there's half a pig's worth of bacon on my table."

"Livvy, darling, I know how long it's been since your vagina was properly used, shitty doesn't come close to describing how bad I feel about clam jamming you."

The mouthful of juice Fin had in his mouth ends up sprayed all over my kitchen counter and he starts hacking up half a lung. Thankfully, Josie remembers how to behave in front of normal humans and intervenes, slapping him on the back and getting him to sit down at the table.

It's bittersweet sitting down to what at this point is effectively brunch; I eat with Mark and Josie all the time but it's usually just the three of us. Mark never brings his bed-mates to meet his friends and Josie has had a long run of boyfriends who've barely passed the three-week mark so they never made the dinner table cut.

Fin rests his hand on the far side of my chair and I lean back slightly so it feels like he's cradling me while we eat. It's a new and interesting sensation. Fin is so much broader than I am, that he makes me feel small. Even though I'd lost most of my weight when I was with Rob and he supported me the whole time, he was only a few inches taller and wider than me, so I never really got that experience of being wrapped up in his arms and feeling delicate. The niggling feeling of guilt that I fit snugly into Fin's side better than I did Rob has me moving uncomfortably. I feel like I should move away from his side. I'm cheating on Rob's memory sitting here having brunch, laughing and joking. He should be here with us. Fin's hand squeezing my waist and pulling me closer to him pulls me from my melancholy. "Where'd you go?" he whispers in my ear.

"I'll fill you in later."

"You know, I'm gonna hold you to all these 'laters' – you owe me some stories."

I know I should be considering how much I'm actually going to tell him but the feel of his morning stubble scratching my ear and my cheek as he whispers in my ear has me squirming in my seat and hoping I don't leave a wet patch on my kitchen chair.

The conversation eventually turns towards rugby, as it often does, and more recently about the funding situation. "I can't believe they're still going to cut our budget. It's ridiculous, they don't support all the sports equally. We have to win this season or we're never going to be able to fight this."

"Why're they going so hard on you guys anyway?"

"A few years ago we were doing really well, moving up the league. We've always had a lot of supports in the student body and plenty of past students come to play in the showcase games." I realise I'm leaning forward in my seat getting worked up about the injustice of university politics.

"But we lost one of our best players and the guys took it really hard. We started losing more matches but we were all still really close and upped our charity work. We got a lot of positive press and people started asking why we were still running our games out of a sports building that needed to be sent back to the firey pits of hell in the seventies." Mark mentioning Rob as one of their best players hits me with another wave of guilt. I need to tell Fin about Rob and sooner rather than later. Even Mark is watching what he says now and I'm not comfortable making my friends lie, even if it's by omission.

"It meant the press the university was getting was pretty negative, while all the stories about the rugby team praised their team spirit and selflessness. Now they're looking for any excuse to reduce funding so they have an automatic excuse not to update the facilities. The newspaper sponsorship is what paid for their uniforms."

Josie chimes in, "All of Livvy's medical equipment she paid for herself. If she didn't volunteer as medic, there wouldn't be one."

"How did you end up as a medic on the rugby team?"

"Mark and I met when I changed schools for my senior years and we decided to take our show on the road by going to the same university. I went to a few matches to support him when we were freshers and after a player got injured in a pretty bad tackle I had to put my first aid training to use and it just kinda stuck." I finish on a shrug because I really don't want to get into the details of how that player happened to be Rob and looking after him was what started our relationship.

"That's ridiculous! I signed up at the start to help you out Mark, and let's be honest, who's gonna turn down the opportunity to bust some heads on the pitch. But now I'm all in, I hate politics. It's got no place on the rugby pitch and it's got no place in university decisions."

"If we can win this season and get the team back on top then they'll have to build us a new centre, where we can actually train during winter without running the risk of losing a toe, or other appendages that are much more important." Mark protectively cups his junk, because even theoretical talk of penis amputation due to frostbite is enough for his boys to get sympathy pains.

"Well our next match is in a week, so we'll massacre them and anyone else who gets in our path. There's no way we're giving these assholes an excuse to screw us." Fin's muscles start to bulge as he gets more worked up. It's amazing how passionate he is about this. He only joined the team a few weeks ago but he seems to have been absorbed into the family with minimal fuss. The fact that he cares about the injustice of the situation enough to get riled up, speaks volumes.

Conversation eventually turns to plans for the week. Fin is interviewing the minister for tourism and taking a tour of Stormont – the country's political centre. Mark is doing a write up of the restaurants he and Fin have visited the past couple of weeks and planning a double-page spread to coincide with the week-long Food Week tourist festival. Josie has her normal ten to six shift in the beauty clinic that she manages. "With Halloween this week we are officially mid-semester and I get to have Thursday through to Tuesday off work. Although I'm hoping I might bump into the Dean this week. He usually likes to do a walk around just before a holiday. If I see him I'm going to speak to him again about the rugby team."

"Livvy, don't. It's not worth the hassle you're going to get from him. He already knows what side your allegiance is on there's no point rubbing his nose in it," Mark interjects.

"I'm not rubbing his nose in anything, Mark. I'm just going to point out to him how unfair it is and hint at how it would be very bad publicity for the university if word were to get out." There's not a doubt in my mind that there's a very devilish smirk on my face right now.

"You stand up for what you believe in, darling, but don't let him bully you because of it." Fin's jaw is set like granite, the idea of that happening obviously displeasing to him.

"Don't you worry. I've had my fill of people bullying me and I'm not going to let Dean McKay walk all over me." I give him a quick kiss on the nose because all this talking means my pancakes are getting cold and my stomach thinks my throat's been cut.

We finish eating every last scrap of pancake, bacon and eggs. Having sex all night really gives you an appetite, apparently. Mark and Josie don't need to be given the hint and make their way home as soon as the dishes are done. Fin seems to have unleashed something because all I really want to do is jump and grind on his lap. The fact that his shirt is unbuttoned enough to show just the tip of chest hair makes me want to run my fingers through it, while I'm grinding on his lap. The lust must be written all over my face because he beckons me over with nothing more than a lift of his chin and pat on his thigh. Hell, he doesn't have to tell me twice. I practically trip over my feet getting to him quickly enough.

Through no choice of my own, my lips seem to be magnetically attracted to his jaw. I start running my lips and flicking my tongue against the column of his throat and up to his jawline. I'm rewarded with a growl and his hands at the small of my back pulling me down on top of his already hard cock. My teeth find the lobe of his ear and I alternate between sucking and biting until I suddenly find myself mid-air and landing on the kitchen table.

Fin growls, "Fuck it," and pulls me to the edge of the table while his hands snake up the back of my vest top and unclip my bra. While Fin's mouth plunders mine, nipping, licking and sucking; my hands finally get to unbutton his shirt and run my fingers over his chest and through his chest hair. I run my nails over his torso, the muscles flexing as I make my way down towards the promised land. My journey abruptly gets interrupted when Fin pulls away and brings my top up over my head, the fabric trailing across my skin and the cooler air flushing me with a wave of chills, anticipating what's about to come.

Fin has my bra whipped off; my nipples immediately standing to attention as I peel his shirt from his shoulders. My hands follow and I scratch my nails gently down the toned flesh. I softly kiss his collarbone and keep kissing down his chest making sure to detour to both his nipples, scoring lightly with my teeth. Fin growls, his fingers tangling in my hair, he pulls me back using my hair to direct me and lies me flat on the kitchen table.

Fin grabs my cotton shorts by the crotch and pulls them down just to my knees. He clips the leg of his chair with his foot and pulls it up behind him. "Time for my treat, Olivia." Lifting my legs up he locks my knees by the shorts behind his head, simultaneously opening me up for him and ensuring I can't move. With his hands pushing my thighs apart Fin drops his head and with no warning, starts feasting on my pussy. He nibbles and licks at my clit every so often delving his tongue inside me; switching it up just enough that I don't know what he's going to do next. I feel like I've been set onto a slow boil and I can feel the pressure building. He picks up the pace and I can't get any traction because my knees are trapped. I need more. Something, anything more. Just when I'm ready to scream in frustration Fin thrusts two fingers inside me as he uses all his suction on my clit. I really do scream; I scream a long stream of nonsense that calls on every deity and a couple of cartoon characters.

I feel my walls still twitching when Fin hooks his fingers inside of me, rubbing the small bundle of nerves while his thumb works on the small bundle outside. I'm really seeing the up side of Fin being ambidextrous when he keeps working me with one hand and with the other grabs a condom. Putting the condom between his teeth Fin lifts and lowers my legs, never once stopping the attention with the other hand. He quickly rids himself of his trousers kicking them over to the ever increasing pile of clothes we've shucked.

Fin must be able to feel me getting more worked up from switching his rubbing to thrusting and speedily sheathes himself. I'm ready to mount him like a fucking mule at this point. I don't want to come again without his cock inside me.

Finally, finally, he slides inside me to the hilt, with virtually no resistance – I'm just that wet at this point.

"So tight, so fucking tight."

Fin starts moving faster, every thrust rocking into me pushing me higher and moving the table at the same time. He lifts both my legs to his shoulders and I lock my ankles behind his head. I can immediately feel the difference, what was already a tight fit becomes even snugger; each inch filling me to the brim. Bending forward Fin changes his trajectory and takes my nipple in his mouth while his finger squeezes and rubs the other. "Jesus, Jesus Christ, Fin." I feel myself getting ready to explode and try desperately to grab on to the edges of the table as Fin picks up even more speed. *This man is a fucking machine.*

"Yes, Olivia, that's it, I can feel you getting tighter, getting ready to milk my fucking cock. You want me to blow inside you don't you? You want my cock coming so deep inside you, you can feel it."

His dirty talk is enough to push me over the edge, my neck arching and my eyes rolling so far back in my head I'm surprised I can't see my brain.

"Fuck yes, that's it, milk my cock, my filthy, filthy girl. Take everything, yes," on a growl Fin comes with me, holding himself tight, every single inch of his rock-hard cock inside me.

When I relax back down on the table, Fin lowers my legs and whether it's from the position or the orgasm I can't feel the damn things. Fin kisses my closed eyes, my nose and my mouth sweetly while he slowly slips out of me. I lie there for who the fuck cares how long just enjoying my post-orgasm buzz while Fin disposes of the condom and pours me a glass of wine and grabs a beer for himself. He sets them down on the coffee table and I like his thinking, because while my legs are still like jelly this table is starting to become more than a little uncomfortable.

"Come on, darling, let's get you warmed up and somewhere a bit softer."

"Mmmm," is about all I can manage in response at this point.

With a chuckle, Fin struts over and slides his hands under my knees and shoulders. His cold hands from the drinks making me squeal and laugh. Somehow he lifts me up as if I weigh nothing and carries me over to the sofa. He sits and then lies down, keeping me in his arms the entire time. I stretch out so I'm lying partly on the sofa and partly on Fin my head resting on his chest and my leg wrapped around his thigh.

I can feel myself falling asleep to the rhythmic rise and fall of Fin's chest. The gentle stroke of his knuckles rubbing up and down my back has me wanting to purr like a kitten. "So, Olivia, it's later."

I feel every muscle stiffen in anticipation of what he's going to say next. "Shh, it's okay, darling, it's not the Spanish Inquisition." He keeps running his hand along my spine; I can feel him willing my muscles to relax. I take a few breaths hoping to clear my head and fend off the impending anxiety.

"Yeah, it's later. But let me sit up if we're going to do this." I pull myself up on the couch and Fin immediately takes my hand in his. The grounding sensation of my hand dwarfed by his actually slows my heart that had been doing a pretty good impersonation of a hummingbird.

"So, where do you want us to start?"

"Us? I thought this was going to be you getting me to spill the beans."

"No, Livvy. I don't expect you to talk to me about your life if I'm not willing to give up a bit of my own."

I'm taken aback because, honestly, I thought this was going to be all about me having to unearth everything. "Okay, so you're originally from Northern Ireland, what made you move away?" Honestly, it's been bugging me. I want to know how long after I moved schools he ran away down south.

"Well, I was having a few issues in and out of school, so when the opportunity came up to go stay with my cousins outside of Dublin, I took it. I spent my last two years of high school there and decided to go to uni down there too." How has he managed to answer my question but leave me with about twenty more? "I've always enjoyed art and photography, but when I first moved I was dealing with some stuff and I found the best way for me to process was behind a camera. I was able to combine journalism and photography at Trinity and I decided that was the career for me. It meant I could get paid for doing what I love." I remember only getting to see a few of Fin's photos when we were in school but he always had a camera with or on him. For him to finally have the confidence to put his photos out there in public is amazing. "So, do you want to tell me about what really happened helping out with the rugby team or how you ended up being on your own for the past two years?"

"To be honest, those two stories are one and the same." I can see the confusion on his face and realise I'm going to have to tell him pretty much everything. The thought of laying this all out doesn't seem as traumatising as I thought it would. This'll be the first time I've actually told the story from start to finish. The paralysing fear I was expecting doesn't seem to come.

"I went to senior school with Mark and we both came to Belfast U together. You know how someone got injured at the match, well that person was Rob McNeill, the team's number eight. When he got injured I had to look after him and we got to talking. I was dealing with some of my own stuff from school, Rob and Mark helped me with it, a lot. Through all of that, Rob and I ended up dating. You can fast forward a few years, I got my degree and released my first novel. After I graduated I got a job as a teaching fellow at the university and worked my way through my Master's degree and released another couple of books. I had an interview at the university to get a job as a full time lecturer rather than just a teaching fellow. Rob and I had arranged to meet for dinner in the city but when I got to the restaurant to tell him I got the job, he wasn't there and he didn't show up."

When I reach for my glass for some liquid courage, Fin wraps his arm around my waist so I have his warmth pressed against me for what will be one of the hardest parts of this story. "He was making his way to the restaurant down a pedestrian zone when some, idiot, decided to drive home after having a few drinks at the end of work." Fin's grip on me tightens and I know he's starting to connect the dots in my story. "They apparently didn't realise they were driving into a pedestrian zone because it had only changed recently and they were too hammered to see the signs, or Rob."

"I'm so sorry, Livvy, he's the rugby player Mark was talking about, wasn't he?"

"Yeah, that was Rob. Everybody took it really hard."

"I'm not surprised, to lose your boyfriend like that must've been devastating."

"I really wish I could say I was finished."

Fin envelopes me in his arms, his scent and warmth staving off the chill that was starting to take root from retelling one of the darkest moments in my life. "That's enough, you don't need to say any more."

"No, but I do. Don't you understand? I've never told anyone this from start to finish because everyone I'm close with was in my life when it happened. I can't escape it, even when I want to for just a little while, everyone still looks at me with that knowing look."

"Okay, sweetheart, okay. Finish your story, take your time."

"Rob's parents live a good few hours away, and what I didn't know was that Rob had named me as his next of kin. So I had to go and identify his body and collect his belongings. It turns out dinner that night wasn't just going to be about whether I got my job or not. I found an engagement ring in amongst his things." I can't hold in the tears anymore and bury my face in Fin's neck while my crying wracks my body. I know it should feel wrong crying about my fiancé on another man's shoulder but it doesn't, and I can't bring myself to pull away from his comfort.

Chapter Ten

Since I'm off today and tomorrow for the mid-semester break Fin has planned another special outing through the NI Tourist Board. I know we're heading out to dinner afterwards but Fin warned me there would be a fair bit of walking for the first part of the night so I've teamed up my black leather Chuck Taylors with my outfit hoping that it covers the best of both worlds.

I'm eagerly waiting for Fin when he pulls up outside in a taxi. I grab my long cardigan because Northern Ireland in October is colder than a witch's tit. When I open the door Fin is already waiting for me, arm extended. Wrapping my arm in his, he gives me a swift, deep kiss before we walk down to the taxi.

"So, do I get to find out where we're going yet?" Honestly, patience is not my strong point and not knowing is killing me.

"Nope," Fin pops, not even attempting to hide his evil grin. He knows it's driving me crazy and he's loving it. We're only in the taxi about ten minutes when we turn up into the north of the city. The tall, foreboding stone wall of Crumlin Road Gaol slowly emerges and something tells me this is where Fin has us going for our date. It's certainly not a conventional choice.

A tour guide is waiting for us at the gates of the jail. As the taxi comes to a stop, he walks over and opens my door. Fin doesn't look best pleased that someone's gotten there before him.

The tour guide leads us into the prison and as soon as we walk into the main atrium where all the wings fan out, the change in atmosphere is palpable. My hand seeks out Fin's as I feel every hair on the nape of my neck rise. We're directed through an old cell which has been staged to represent the original cells. Being the only people in this prison, the hanging artificial bulbs our only source of light adds a paranormal hue to everything in sight. Fin isn't using the flash on his camera so he can capture the ambiance. It's disturbing but manageable.

However, our next stop is the hanging room. In the small high-ceilinged room, the gallows are still in place. Over a dozen men met their end in this room. Not necessarily all of them guilty. Nearly all are buried in the grounds, so even in death they couldn't escape this place. Even the most cynical visitor couldn't be in this room and not sense the evil in here. I swear, I feel the hair at the side of my ear move and that's it for me, I can't take it anymore. I have to get out of this room. My hand tightens in Fin's and he takes my lead by excusing us and heading back out into the corridor.

"I'm sorry, Olivia, I thought this would be fun. Something creepy for Halloween." He looks genuinely perplexed, unsure of what my reaction is going to be.

I try my best to force a smile. "It's fine Fin, honestly, I just wasn't expecting it to be quite so oppressive. It's rather apropos for Halloween, though."

"Our hour is nearly up anyway and I have more than enough for my article. We can finish up. Are you okay to wait out here for a minute? I didn't get any pictures in the last room and it's one of their prize spots on the tour."

The thought of waiting out here on my own doesn't thrill me, but I know that Fin has a job to do. I nod and give him a tight smile hoping he read my thoughts and makes it as quick as possible.

Fin ducks back into the room and no sooner is he in than the tour guide comes out. "Your friend didn't want you waiting out here on your own. He says he'll be done in just a minute."

I exhale a sigh of relief, trust Fin to think of sending the tour guide out to me, leaving himself in that horrible place. True to his word it's less than a minute later when Fin steps back out zipping up his camera bag. The tour guide leads us the quick way back, pointing out in passing where the governor's chambers were. Fin thanks him profusely for the solo tour and promises a very interesting write up. I breathe my first relaxing breath of fresh air once we step outside. The cool autumn air cleansing my skin and my lungs as Fin calls up our ride.

We take the taxi to the restaurant for dinner, leaving the creepy vibes of the prison behind us. The second I step out onto cobblestones I know where we are. This pedestrianised area of Belfast is amazing and you can find pretty much every ethnicity of food here. I'm eternally thankful that I chose to wear my high-tops tonight because high heels and cobblestones are not friends.

Fin takes my hand to help me out of the car, apparently not impressed that I chose to let myself out of the taxi myself. Fitting me into his side, Fin leads us to a beautiful French restaurant that's tucked away in between two terraced houses that hold businesses. D'Arcy's has the most amazing food and all its staff, including the chefs, are French. I'm always dubious at restaurants when the waiters have accents, I'm convinced they're putting it on so they condescend you without you realizing it.

The dining room is about two table lengths wide but long so there's enough room between the tables to keep your conversations private. The damask wallpaper and hanging candelabras give the room a cosy ambiance. The only real light in the room is from the candelabras and the candles on the tables. No one could look bad in this room. It's like walking into a snapchat filter.

The maître d' shows us to our table. The tables are just the right size that we don't need to sit side by side to be close, plus I get to play footsie with him under the tablecloth. Fin orders the wine for us, no chance for the waiter to even try to be condescending, I leave this entirely up to Fin. I don't care what colour it is or what its alcohol content is as long as it doesn't taste like vinegar. Once the waiter leaves we start to look through the menus. It's entirely in French so I'm piecing together bits and pieces from memories of previous meals at restaurants. I'm seriously contemplating asking for a menu with pictures just so I don't end up ordering deep fried snails or something.

Fin somehow uses his freaky intuition to notice that I'm having issues and starts translating the meals for me. He gives their name in French first. The next time we're alone I'm going to have him roll his tongue like that again, but not in his mouth or mine. I decide to go for something different and order moules marinière. Mussels cooked in white wine and cream. As if that wasn't heavenly enough, they also come with a side of fries, baguette and butter. I'm going to have to control my drool. The waiter very efficiently comes over to our table, pouring our glasses of wine and asking for our food order.

All of a sudden Fin starts ordering oysters. Not something I signed up for. Before I even get a chance to voice my concerns, Fin directs his attention to me. "I've only ordered a half dozen, just in case you don't like them. I wasn't going to order them in case you were allergic to shellfish, but since you're good with mussels I figured you'd be safe."

"I might be safe with shellfish but I've never had oysters before. From what I remember of seeing them I'm not sure they're the sort of thing I want in my mouth."

Fin leans forward over the modestly-sized table, we're almost nose to nose. "Would I ever put something in your mouth you couldn't handle, Olivia? Plus, they're a renowned aphrodisiac, not that we need any help in that department." He winks and sits back in his seat obviously pleased with himself.

It doesn't take long for our oysters to arrive. Six oysters that look like grey rocks cut in half. All placed strategically over a tray of crushed ice. They're served with little pots of different coloured sauces and one filled with freshly sliced lemon wedges. The next few minutes consist of Fin trying unsuccessfully to convince me to try an oyster. After a demonstration of how simple it apparently is to eat an oyster, I concede. Squeezing a large helping of lemon juice onto one of the slippery little buggers I think of it like taking a solid shooter. I open my throat and throw the oyster back. The lemon juice kills off the majority of any other possible tastes and it's surprisingly not too bad. We work our way through the remaining oysters, trying one with the hot sauce and then another with some sort of vinegar reduction. Fin bursts into laughter every time I swallow one because according to him my face when the acidity registers is hilarious.

Out of the blue, the door opens in a flurry of pink and as soon as I notice who's walked in, any food in my stomach sours. It was a huge test that Fin didn't recognise me. I'd made a point of changing pretty much everything about my appearance. It was a new name, new me. But the blonde bitch that's picking her way down the room right now spent the majority of her time at school in my face, tormenting me. Maybe if I hope and wish hard enough she'll just teeter on by in her five-inch stilettos and not even notice us.

But of course, if life has taught me anything, it's that you never get what you really want. In fact, the more you want it, the further it slips out of your reach. It's no surprise that just as soon as Fin and I were feeling relaxed and more comfortable together, a hurricane from our past had to come blowing in. Hurricane Fiona.

Fiona McCormick was queen of the Stepford Bitches. They moved like gazelles around the school halls; a herd of long neck sociopaths looking for the nearest weak prey. More often than not, that weak prey was me. When they weren't openly ripping people to shreds, they were executing perfect jellyfish stings – it wouldn't be until after you walked away from the conversation that you realised how badly you'd been stung.

Fiona prances up to our table and I can already feel myself recoiling back, attempting to shrink into my body so maybe she won't see me. *Maybe she's like a T-rex and if I don't move she can't see me.* "Fin, darling," she drawls with some fake quasi-British accent. It would be almost worth exposing my real identity just to point out that she grew up in Northern Ireland like the rest of us and no one's buying her psycho Mary Poppins routine.

Fin, always the gentleman, *though this time I wish he'd act like a bastard,* stands to greet her. "Fiona, how are you?" He holds his hand out to her, at least he isn't sweeping her off her feet or anything. Fiona bats his hand away and steps up to him wrapping her spindly arms around him and kissing both his cheeks. I'm filled with the strange sensation of wanting to snap her arms off her body and beat her with them.

"Oh, shush now, Fintan. Shaking hands, really. Old friends like us need a much more intimate greeting." While apparently some of us can create a whole new persona and life for ourselves, others prefer to remain the same self-centred vapid idiots they always were. Fin takes a step back with an uncomfortable chuckle.

"Um, yeah. Nice to see you too." Fin takes another step backwards, as if he's about to sit back down. Fiona doesn't give him a chance though, she just steps right up to him again, her hands running down his chest, my chest! *Who the fuck does she think she is?*

"You should give me a shout later, when you're finished with your sister." She finishes her path down his chest, her fake, blood red nails leaving a trail of scratches down the fabric of his shirt. Her jibe scratches at me; even now, all these years later, she manages to leave me mute in the wake of her destruction.

Fin removes her hand and drops it mid-air. "Actually, Fiona, I'm on a date. As you already know, since you also know I don't have a sister." This woman has a serious set of balls on her, she just smiles and laughs it off, as if he didn't just catch her being a grade-A bitch.

"Oh, of course, how silly of me. You're on a date." She blatantly gives me the side-eye. "I just assumed from the amount of carbs on the table that it couldn't possibly be a date. But then again, some of us like to take better care of ourselves." Her eyes track me up and down, well what she can see of me above the table; she's clearly finding me lacking and not making any attempt to hide it.

Her venomous gaze must've been the last straw because Fin barks, "That's enough Fi, just go to your table." I wish I could say Fin rejecting her made me feel better, but my mind focuses on the nickname he uses. He never called her Fi when we were in school. Hell, he was the one that helped to come up with the name Stepford Bitches. Did she sink her claws into him after I ran away with my tail between my legs? I was always convinced she liked Fin, and my friendship with him fuelled the flames of her hatred of me. She couldn't understand why someone like Fin could be interested in spending time with someone like me. Fin and I never officially dated. We were best friends who also made out on more than one occasion. But we both had so much stress in our personal lives that we used each other as solace. We didn't talk about what was going on outside of our own little bubble. When I was with Fin, even just in his presence it was enough to quiet all the noise of life. He was my safe harbour and I was his. Back then, Fin was good looking but he hadn't grown into himself yet. When you looked at him though, really looked at him, past the pain in his eyes and the overgrown hair, anyone could see the beautiful man he would grow into.

That one word, Fi, hurts me more than all of Fiona's barbs. It tells me that at some point, after he was ripped from my life, he became close to her. How close I don't think I really want to know; I don't think I could stomach the thought of them together.

Thankfully, Fiona takes heed of Fin's tone and starts to move away. Not without one, last parting shot of course. "When you're ready to move up the food chain, Fin, give me a call." Fin sits back down, looking part sheepish, part pissed off.

"I'm sorry about that," he says while replacing his napkin. I genuinely don't know what to say, I feel like a masochist, wanting to know no matter how much it may hurt.

"Old friend?"

"No, she's more someone I...tolerated. We went to school together and I haven't seen her for a few years. Since the last time I came back up North for a quick trip home." Again, I'm left with more questions from his answers. He must take my silence as a request to continue. "Yes, she's always been a bit bitchy. That's one of the reasons we've never really been friends." He stated that a lot more politely than I would have. "Let's move on and get back to our dinner, shall we?" Not a question, a command, and hell if it doesn't help take the edge off the friction I'm feeling after our run in with Fiona.

I pick at most of what's left of my dinner, the distaste of our early encounter ruining my palette. Thank God for wine. I probably have a glass too many for the little I've eaten, but my hunger ran off along with my backbone as soon as the baby-pink clusterfuck arrived at our table.

If Fin notices that I'm not myself, he at least has the decency not to comment on it. We slowly start to get back into our groove with the conversation somehow swinging round to ranking the best Star Trek captains. Fin pays for dinner and won't even let me put my hand to my purse.

We make our way out and make the short crossing of a few feet to the Duke of York pub. The bar is heaving with bodies but the atmosphere is tangible. There are license plates of all origins and names nailed to the walls. Old tin ads and slogans decorate every available inch, filling the bar with age and history. We manage to make our way to the bar, Fin's arm protectively wrapped around me ensuring I don't get bumped or covered in beer.

The bar looks and sounds like something out of an old Irish tourist advert. There's a two-piece band in the corner, one man in a leather jacket strumming out folk music on an electro-acoustic guitar and his partner in crime in a flap cap and tweed coat playing a bodhrán, adding the drum beat to his music. All we need is a toothless alcoholic and the cliché will be complete.

Fin manages to snag a table near to the musicians. The beer is perfectly cold and slips down my throat far too easily. We sit there nursing our way through a couple of beers, listening and swaying to the music. Not talking, not even trying to communicate. Just gently moving our bodies, Fin's arm relaxing around the back of my chair, my free hand resting against his thigh that occasionally tightens and relaxes. As I start to get too relaxed from the melodic beat of the music, our synchronised movements and the alcohol, Fin starts to stand up. "Come on, sleepyhead, let's get you home."

Making our way outside, arms cinched around each other; the cold is brisk and does a good job of sobering me up as we head to the waiting line of taxis. My gaze shoots to Fin's when he gives the driver his address and not mine. "I figured it was about time you got to see my place." The importance of him letting me into his space is apparent in the way his grip on my hand tightens and releases.

Fin's apartment isn't actually too far from my house. We're both in the outskirts of Belfast, maybe only a ten-minute walk from each other. The willow trees surrounded by black iron fleur-de-lis railings every hundred yards illustrates that we're entering one of the higher-end suburbs. The taxi pulls up in front of a three-storey Georgian-style townhouse, the terracotta slates and black detailing in stark contrast to the white. The building is a lot bigger than I'd been expecting. I don't know why I was imagining him still being in a two-up, two-down little house like the one at home. He must be on similar money to Mark, so why wouldn't he be in a fancy apartment building?

Fin, again, pays for the ride. I'm going to have to point out to him that as a lecturer I'm probably on similar money to him and can actually pay for a few things myself. Fin opens up and lets us in, the palm of his hand warm on the small of my back as he takes me up the two flights of stairs to his apartment. There's only one door up here so Fin must have the entire top floor to himself. As the door opens I'm astounded by the space in front of me. While the apartment itself seems to be inviting with its cream panelling and pine flooring; there is a distinctly masculine aura to the room. There are no family photographs or quaint touches that announce the space as Fin's. It's a generic high-end apartment that shows no signs of life, apart from a coffee cup in the sink and a giant TV in the living room.

Fin leads me into the apartment and deposits me on the large, black, leather sectional sofa. I immediately sink down into the soft leather. My body is so tired but with our altercation earlier and finally getting to see where lives my mind's buzzing. Fin comes back from the kitchen with two glasses of red wine. The liquid's deep burgundy visible from the side lamp Fin lit on his way to the kitchen.

"A small night-cap, before we head to bed." Fin clinks glasses with mine and we both savour a sip of the robust wine.

"I can't believe I'm this tired," I manage to say before I'm engulfed in a full body yawn.

"Yeah, I find when I have to have any dealings with bitches it takes it out of me too," Fin adds.

I'm not sure what way to take his statement until I look up and see him trying to hide a smile.

"Yeah, she was pretty…full on." *Honestly, what else can I say other than she's a stark raving psycho?*

"She's a lot of work. If you think tonight was bad you should've seen her when we were in school. She was a raving nut job. Anybody who got their dick wet with her needed to have their head examined. She'd go full bunny-boiler at the drop of a pin."

I manage to snort laugh red wine out my nose, just getting my hand up in time to save my clothes.

"Ok, that's it. You're officially cut off," Fin laughs as he takes my glass away and places it in the sink with his. Raising both his hands out to me he helps me out of the sofa cushions that were becoming way too comfortable and leading me up the small set of stairs to the slightly elevated portion of his apartment.

His bedroom seems like his sanctuary. There are several different cameras sitting out. A sketch book, closed unfortunately. *I'd love to see what his drawing is like now all these years later.* The requisite sports and photography magazines. Still no photographs of people though. There are some very arty prints on the walls, but none of them have a living subject.

"Finished having a good look?"

I spin round expecting Fin to be angry that I'm blatantly taking in all the information about him that I can. But the look on his face isn't one of anger, it's hunger.

"Now I'm going to have *my* good look Livvy."

And that's exactly what he does. After he strips me down and lays me flat on the bed he makes sure that he looks, touches and kisses every inch of my body.

I start to finally fall asleep with Fin's arm as my pillow, thinking about our night.

While it was still thoroughly rigorous, the frantic pace of the other times we've had sex wasn't there. I didn't think it was possible but I think the slow pace to savour the action actually made my orgasms even stronger. I'll be lucky if I can walk in a straight line tomorrow morning.

I make my way to the showers after our teacher forced us to all take a physical in the gym. I would take cross country running over having the senior pupils' training by giving us the Bleep Test and measuring our body fat. I knew I should have come up with some sort of excuse to get out of class. Thankfully this is the last class of the day but it means I'm going to be late to meet Fin. Usually I'm the last to shower and change so I don't give anyone the opportunity to pass comment but this is the first chance I've had to see Fin; he's been rushing home every day this week.

By the time I've made it to the changing room, most pupils seem to have finished and already heading home – I plan to be one of them very soon. I make my way to the corner farthest from the door and closest to the showers. Wrapping my towel around me I start to get undressed as quickly as possible. Focussing on completing my task, I don't notice the pupils coming into the room until I hear the shrill voice that will no doubt follow me to my grave.

"No need to visit the zoo, ladies. We have our very own beached whale right here. Honestly, Bessie, how do you even get out the front door of your house?" They all keep cackling as if this is the height of wit. Fiona will just keep going until she gets bored so I head into one of the cubicles, hoping that she might get fed up waiting to torment me further. I wash quickly, and press my ear against the door. There's nothing but silence and the sound from my own shower.

I pick my way across the floor trying not to make a noise that might make them come back in here. When I reach my changing bag I feel the sensation of dread course through me, as if someone had tipped cold water down my back. My stomach lurches when I reach inside my bag for my clean, dry clothes and come up empty. Just as the recognition sinks in that my clothes are missing, I register the sound of running water. There's still one shower on. Like the dumb blonde in every horror movie ever made, I make my way to the shower in nothing but my birthday suit and a towel. Pulling back on the door the steam rises and escapes. In its wake I see the soaking wet remnants of my clothing. Every last piece of clothing that was in my bag.

I can't hold back the tears when I think about how I'm going to get home. I can't even get home like this. I've learned to stop telling my parents what happens in school. I can't take the pain in my mother's eyes when she knows her baby girl is going through hell and there's nothing she can do about it. She's tried. She's done everything but sue the school. But without any evidence, the school gives their normal mantra: 'Our hands are tied'. Rinse and repeat for another four years.

Desperately wringing as much excess water out of my clothes as I can, I force my body into them, ignoring the chaffing against my skin. I peer out the door hoping that the coast is clear and I can find some way of hiding this from my mother. A hand on my shoulder as I make my stealthy escape has me spinning and squealing in fear.

"Lizzie, what the fuck happened to you?" Fin's face is almost purple with fury as he takes in my appearance. I'm certain I look more like a drowned rat than a schoolgirl at this point. I feel my lip tremble and the tears that had just subsided resurface with a vengeance. "Shh, shh. It's okay my darling. Let's get you home and get you dried off."

"No! No, Fin. My mum can't know. The last time nearly destroyed her. This has to stay between us. Please, please." I desperately grab at the lapels of his coat. She cannot find out about this, I don't know what this would do to her. She's been working under the assumption that things have been going okay.

"Okay, darling, okay. Are you okay to walk to my place?" I can barely hear him as he talks into my hair, running his hand down my hair continuously while the other holds me up. He can feel me nodding my head because he continues, "Okay, let's go darling."

The walk to Fin's house is mercifully short. It's already getting dusky outside and there isn't a light on in Fin's house.

"Where's your family?"

"Dad was talking about taking Mum out for dinner. They must've decided to go. Come on, let's head to the garage, there's a utility room in there with a dryer." Fin unlocks the door and leading me by the hand, works his way through the graveyard of car parts and broken appliances. The flickering neon lights make the place even eerier. Inside the utility room, Fin empties the dryer, passing me sweatpants and a jumper. Judging from the size, they have to be Fin's.

"I'll leave you to get changed." Fin presses some buttons and turns dials. "The dryer's all set up for you. Just pop your clothes in and close the lid."

"You must be the only man I know who knows how to use a dryer."

Fin gives me a sad smile. "I can use a washing machine too." He makes his way to the door. "Get changed before you give yourself pneumonia."

When he closes the door I quickly get undressed and slip on Fin's clothes. Looking down, I notice that they're a little big, but they don't drown me. I wish they would drown me, I'd love nothing more than to feel slight, not weak but dainty. I see women in movies and books and they always talk about being drowned in clothes, how sexy it is. It isn't sexy when the man's clothes are only just too *big for you. The dryer must have only just finished its cycle because there's still a little heat in them and it feel glorious against my skin.*

Fin is leaning against the bar, his head arched upwards, his red converse in stark contrast to the black of the floor. His hands are behind his head and he seems to be deep in thought.

"Thank you. I'm not sure I would've made it home in that condition." Fin rights himself and steps close to me.

"Anytime you need me, darling." He takes my face in his hands and in the next breath, seals his mouth over mine. Washing away all the pain of today, at least for a few moments. "Come on, let's go."

We make our way outside to Fin's back garden. This is our spot. Mrs. Kelly doesn't really spend much time out here. Mr. Kelly mows the lawn but that's all he does back here. The only flowerbeds that are tended to are the two at the front of the house. There's a ten foot trampoline in the far corner. When we were younger, Fin and I would have competitions seeing who could bounce the highest and trying to out-do each other with our stunts. Until Mrs. Kelly needed Fin inside to help with something or other and I would make my way home.

As we got older it became less about bouncing and more about having a small space that was ours. The trees that line the length of the property give us just enough shelter that we feel removed from the rest of the world around us. The green netting our force field against the trials and tribulations that wait outside for us.

Fin opens up the trampoline and helps me climb in first. He follows after and we assume our positions, lying on the canvas, staring up at the blanket of stars above us.

"You don't have to take this, Lizzie, you know that right?" I guess there's no easing into this conversation.

"Fin, you remember what happened the last time I tried to stand up to them. I was still washing marinara sauce out of my hair a week later."

Rolling onto his side his eyes find mine, "I remember; I just wish there was something more I could do for you. I wish we had all the same classes so I could keep an eye on you all the time."

"You do enough for me, Fin. Just being here for me, that's all I need." Fin wraps his arms around me, pulling me closer, so my head is on his chest, feeling his heart beat under my palm.

"You know I love you, Lizzie, you're my best friend. Don't ever forget that, okay?" He squeezes me tighter.

"I won't forget Fin, I just don't know how much longer I can take this." Something is going to have to give. I need to leave or try to find a way to get Fiona to leave me alone for good. I still have

two and a half years left at St Ignacious. I can't take over two more years of this, but I can't think of any way to stop it. No matter what way I look at it, I can't see a way out and I can't see a way to survive it. The tears that track my cheeks cool immediately with the night air. It might not be able to help, but just lying here in Fin's arms and letting it all go is making me feel a little better.

The next few hours, before I sneak home around the side of the house, are spent crying my heart out onto Fin's shoulder with what we thought was only the stars watching us.

"Olivia, Olivia, what's wrong?"

I startle awake to Fin leaning over me, nose to nose. I realise I'm crying when Fin begins wiping the tears from my face. "I'm fine, just a dream."

"That's one hell of a dream, darling. Wanna tell me about it?"

"No, honestly, it'll pass. They always do." Fin sits up and pulls me into his arms. I focus my eyes on the bedroom wall in front of me until Fin places two fingers under my chin and turns my face towards him.

"Ya get these often?"

"No, not so much anymore." I rest my head back on his chest, fighting back a yawn, the adrenaline starting to recede already.

"What can I do to help?"

"Just hold me for a minute."

We must fall asleep in that position because I wake the next morning still wrapped tightly in Fin's arms.

Chapter Eleven

"The moments that make life worth living are when things are
at their worst and you find a way to laugh."
-Amy Schumer

There's a definite nip to the air this morning as I wrap myself up and make my way to the rugby pitches. Josie's already there waiting like a freaking Godsend with a thermos full of what had better be coffee. We set up at the side of the pitch and I swear it's déjà vu to a few weeks ago, but instead of being filled with apprehension, I'm strangely settled and giddy at the thought of getting to see Fin play again.

We're up against Northern Ireland's only other university today, NIU, it shouldn't be too difficult a match but some of these guys are huge. I wonder if these guys are born huge, my vagina weeps for their mothers' because holy hell, that's got to be a big baby.

Fin, Mark and all of the boys run out, a sea of green and red, Fin looks over and gives me a chin lift and a wink; I can feel the smile tugging at my lips in response. The chuckle coming from my left shoulder tells me Josie can see it too. "You are such a smitten kitten!" she says, nudging my shoulder, nearly making me spill my coffee. I give her a glare suited to near-caffeine-abuse. "Oh lighten up, it wasn't that close to spilling. I know you're not into this thing with Fin 100% but it's nice to see you smile again."

"I smile all the time, you daft cow." I mean really, she makes it sound like I'm a grumpy bitch all the time.

"No, Liv, you really don't. You pretend smile, it's like a shadow of what a real smile should me. Your face knows what it should be doing, and it goes through the motions. But there's no emotion behind it." She gives me a sad smile of her own. "But recently, recently you've been smiling more and even your pretend smiles are becoming more genuine. It's good to see is all."

"Oh." I mean what am I supposed to say to a bombshell like that?

"Come on, we've just won the coin toss, let's watch."

The game kicks off and immediately there's a flurry of activity. The boys aren't holding back today. Thankfully, I'm not needed much in the first half; mostly providing isotonic drinks to the players who run off pitch to vomit last night's drinks. It's worse than usual today, mostly because Halloween is a long celebration for students and they've probably spent the last three days drinking.

Josie uses halftime to run to the campus shop and grab a couple of muffins, as if there's ever an excuse needed for muffins. The steam from our fresh coffees carries the aroma and I can feel my brain cloying for the caffeine hit that the smell signals. Just as the heat warms up my blood and I can start feeling my extremities again, the second half starts up.

NIU have swapped a couple of players for this half and one of them I definitely don't recognise. I'm pretty sure that I would remember coming into contact with a guy that looks like he should be on WWE. His long hair is tied back in a man bun and I've seen thighs that aren't as wide as his neck. It's like someone from the Avengers has lost their way and found themselves on a rugby pitch. From his position he's playing forward which means he's going to be right in the front row for the scrum.

The action is thick and fast this half and by the time ten minutes have gone by, both teams have scored two tries and converted them from three points to seven. We're still winning but the margin in points isn't as wide as I would like it to be. The man mountain makes a break with the ball and I'm struck dumb by the speed of him. How in the hell can he move that fast, carrying that much weight? Fin spots him and starts to mirror his movements, they're parallel on the pitch, both charging towards the try line. Fin has the edge on him speed-wise and starts veering on a path that will directly intercept The Beast. Just as they start sharing the same pitch space, Fin drops his shoulder and throws out his arm. I don't know if it's because he came from the left-hand side or The Beast was more focused on the target but Fin seems to have caught him off-guard. They both go down with a roar and Fin is immediately back on his feet. Ball in his left hand. Ball in the air. Ball flying back at ferocious speed into the safe area of the pitch from Fin's kick that looks like it started last week with the amount of force he put behind it.

It's not until I follow the ball's trajectory and see Mark catch it, that I glance back to the clash of the rugby players. Fin's right arm is hanging by his side, his teeth gritting with every step he makes back towards the match. He stops by Humungo and holds out his left hand to help him up. With a lot of blustering and blowing both men are back on their feet and run-walking up the pitch. Before my brain catches up with my body, I'm running onto the pitch and running my eyes over Fin assessing what sort of damage he's done to himself.

"Livvy, what the fuck," Fin growls as I try to touch his arm and see what range of movement he has.

"Let me see, Fin," I make another pass at his arm and as he tries to wrench it free he cries out, he's obviously in pain. I'd lay money on it being a typical man thing and not wanting to show weakness. Well, I'm not giving him another option. "You come off this pitch right now, Fintan Kelly and let me check out your arm or so help me God I will throw a hissy fit the likes of which you have never seen!" I give him my best deadly stare, usually saved for students who have crossed my path for the wrong reasons. He finally relents with a nod and follows me to the sidelines just before the ref was about to stop play.

His shoulder is starting to swell already and there are subtle blue and purple hues forming on the skin. I can tell from his range of movement it isn't dislocated but it's definitely not right either. I convince Fin to sit the rest of the game out and to let me ice his shoulder.

By the end of the match and a lot of grumbling from Fin about missing the action, we've won by one try and Fin has a bit more movement back in his shoulder. I'm still not happy with it but Fin is determined to leave going to the hospital for later, if it gets worse.

I caught the bus to the match, but Fin drove and given his limited movements, I'm going to have to drive his car for him. Mark comes out with Fin's gym bag and puts it in the car. Giving me a wan smile he heads back in to get changed. Josie and I get a begrudging Fin in the car and I take him home, to his home. I figure I can walk back to mine since I now know where he lives.

Once we get inside, Fin beelines for the bathroom and comes out with a couple of pills in his hand. I quirk my eyebrow and he explains, "Old painkillers. They make me a bit drowsy but they'll make the pain easier to manage for a while."

I know there's no point arguing with him so I fetch him a glass of water and then get him situated on one of his recliners. My plan to make him something to eat is scuppered when he grabs the back of my shirt with his left hand and pulls me back to the chair. Reaching down, he pops the button and we both go sailing backwards where I'm now reclined half on top of the left side of Fin's body, half on the chair. "Just lay here with me a little while," he mumbles as he buries his nose in my hair, "how do you always smell so good?" *I think it's safe to say the meds are kicking in.* Giggling when he starts actively sniffing around my ear and hair, woofing and pretending to be a dog; it quickly becomes a moan when he licks the column of my neck and bites down lightly on my ear lobe. His moans become a groan of pain when I shift on him to get in position to go to town on his neck. His cry of pain is enough to bring me back to reality and I immediately jump off him aware that I may have just made his injury worse. "No, no, no I'm good, I'm good, get that gorgeous ass back up here."

"Nuh uh, I'm getting some more ice for that shoulder because you're not gonna be able to take any more pills for a while." I grab a disposable ice pack and some freeze gel from my kit and go back to Fin, taking my frustrations out on the ice pack, activating the freezing process.

While Fin settles in with the ice pack in front of the TV, I have a nosey about his kitchen. I'm not ashamed to nosey, you can tell a lot about someone from their kitchen. It looks like Fin must do some cooking at home because he has all the staples and his cupboards have a reasonable selection of soups and noodles. His bread isn't too old so I make some soup and sandwiches for lunch and to hopefully line his stomach before he has to take some more painkillers.

Fin wasn't lying when he said he was pretty ambidextrous because from the look of it, if he hadn't been high as a kite on pain pills he wouldn't be having any issue eating his soup. His movements get progressively stiffer as the meal goes on. By the time I'm clearing up, his ice pack is body temperature and just unwanted weight on his shoulder.

Grabbing the freeze gel I pop the chair upright and straddle Fin's hips. There are definitely some advantages to this injury. Fin gets the idea and starts to help me lift his shirt. My thumbs trail over his abs and the small smattering of hair along his chest. It's just enough to add colour and for his happy trail to direct me where to go. *As if I don't already know.*

I start applying the gel and massaging it into his shoulder. I make sure to work on any knots and tension I can feel; Fin's head is at the perfect height to my tits as he sits forward to let me get access to his back. Adding more gel to the mix I push downwards on the muscles noting the way his swelling, at least the one at his shoulder, has gone down. The other swelling, however, has gotten much harder in the time I've been working on him.

Fin makes my job considerably harder when he starts kissing and working on my neck. He makes his way down past my collarbone to the tops of my breasts. Any hope I had of keeping focused on my task flies out the window. I kiss my way down past the hair I was so enamoured with, pausing briefly to run my tongue over each of his nipples.

The happy trail points to where I need to be and at the minute there is a beautiful package waiting to be unwrapped at the end. Sliding down Fin's body, I kneel between his feet and peel down his tracksuit bottoms, his solid length bobbing free, already glistening at the tip. Lifting his hip I secure the tracksuit under him and take him in both my hands.

Using the underside of my tongue I tease the tip while stroking up and down at an increasing speed. Just as I take him all in my mouth I move my left hand to his balls pulling ever so gently. I increase speed as I increase the depth into my mouth, now running my tongue along his hard cock with each movement. The fact that he hasn't showered has left a bit of a weird taste but I power on through because I can't get enough of the look on Fin's face every time we make eye contact like this. His hands threading into my hair tells me that I've found the right pace and suction for his liking. But breathing through my nose isn't ideal with the strange taste getting stronger.

It isn't until I start getting a tingling feeling on my lips and Fin starts making frustrated noises that I realise I've made a terrible, terrible mistake. From the look on Fin's face as I jump up and run to the bathroom, he realised at about the same time I did.

I skid into the bathroom and start the tap running, lapping at the water like a dog, trying desperately to get rid of the freeze gel that had been all over my hands and is currently all over my mouth and tongue. Fin's body landing against the door frame while he unsuccessfully stifles his laughs at my current condition has me whipping my head round. I start splashing water at him as punishment for finding my numb mouth so hilarious. But he overpowers me quickly, not once stopping his laugher. I don't know what he finds so funny, if I can't feel my mouth he sure as hell can't feel his dick.

Fin stops laughing long enough to pin my back to his front, his hips holding me tight against the basin. I barely recognise my reflection in the mirror. I've put a little weight back on, but can't seem to bring myself to care. My face is flushed and eyes bright from laughter. He stops and watches me in the mirror. I wonder if he can see what I can see? Leaning down he places a kiss on the nape of my neck and steps away.

I follow him back out to the living room where he's assumed the position from before the freeze gel incident. Extending his arm, he beckons me back over and once I'm situated on his lap again he turns on Netflix and puts on season three of Doctor Who.

I don't know if it's the drugs that makes Fin content to lie there, but I'm happy to stay right here until Fin needs more meds; content to simply watch David Tennant and feel Fin's heart beating under my palm. That is exactly what we do.

Chapter Twelve

'The worst sin - perhaps the only sin - passion can commit, is to be joyless.'
- Dorothy L Sayers

Despite the misapplication of freeze gel, between anti-inflammatories and ice packs, Fin's shoulder gains a lot more movement and a lot less swelling by the time he arrives at my house the next day. When I open the door for him he immediately takes my face in his hands, kissing me breathless whilst walking me backwards against the door. Kicking the door shut on his way he moves his hands to mine and places them above my head, holding them with one hand against the wall.

"You and your freeze gel left me with a serious case of blue balls last night, Olivia." Thrusting his hips against the apex of my thighs with each word he continues, "what are you going to do about it?" The hand not pinning mine moves down my body, cupping my breast and rubbing his thumb roughly over my hardened nipple.

"Oh God," when he pinches my nipple I moan like a whore, "anything you damn well want me to do." Fin's grinding picks up speed as does his ministrations with his hand. There's a serious chance he's going to make me come just by dry humping me against this wall. Just as I start to see lights and hear bells I realise that my doorbell is actually ringing, not the sweet angels of sexual deviation. "Shit, that's dinner."

Fin groans in frustration in my ear. "Cock-blocked by food. I suppose there are worse things."

"Yeah, like numbing cream." I peel myself away from the wall and open the front door. Once I've paid, Fin takes the bag of food from my hands and I go to set the table, making sure I put Fin's cutlery the way he likes it and grab us both a beer.

"What, no chopsticks?" Fin asks as he sits beside me at the table.

"Not unless you want to be covered in the food that flies out of mine."

Replying, "fair enough," Fin tries to hide his smile behind a roll.

We're both too busy enjoying our food for a good few minutes to talk.

"Did you ever bump into the Dean this week by the way?" Fin has managed to inhale most of his plate of food, which was already a hell of a lot heftier serving than mine.

"No. No surprise there, he was nowhere to be seen when I was around. I did meet with a few other faculty members and they've said they'll start coming to the games. They want to show their solidarity. I was thinking if we get a few pictures of them lined up at the front of the crowd in university colours it might go well with the articles."

"Articles? Plural?"

"Yep. Articles, as in I want to run just after the Christmas break stating where we are in the league and implying what will happen if we don't win and don't have the student body backing us."

Fin looks perturbed at my suggestion. "Do you think that's wise, Olivia? You may as well be painting a target on your back. You know they'll know exactly where the article is coming from."

"They'll know it but they won't be able to prove it, so technically they won't be able to do anything to me." It's a no-brainer as far as I'm concerned.

"Just be careful, darling. I find it sexy as all hell that you stand up for what you believe in but you need to make sure you're protecting yourself too."

"You think I'm sexy?" I'm genuinely surprised by this. I've been called a lot of things in my life, but sexy isn't one that comes up often.

"Fuck yes. I think you're sexy all the damn time but when you actually try to be, you're down right irresistible."

"Oh really?" I put his theory to the test and look up at him.

"Olivia," Fin warns, "don't start something you're not ready to finish."

Biting, then running my tongue over my bottom lip I give Fin the innocent ingénue look. "Start what?"

The fire in Fin's eyes has me wanting him to make good on his threat, so I slowly push my chair back and make my way towards the staircase, adding as much swish to my hips as possible.

I leave one shoe at the bottom of the stairs, looking over my shoulder with my best attempt at come-to-bed eyes. I leave its pair halfway up the staircase and kick my superwoman-themed boxers off and leave them on the floor outside my room like a sexy breadcrumb trail.

When Fin follows me into the bedroom I push him down onto the bed and he pulls my dress over my head. Sitting up he kisses the swells of my breasts, pulling each cup down to give him unfettered access to my nipples. I arch back thrusting them in his face, I need more of this now and I'm not afraid to ask for it.

Fin lies back down on the bed and crooks his finger towards me. "Come here, Olivia, I want you to sit on my face."

I can feel my own face burning from the bluntness of his order and the thought of having to climb up his body. That sort of position is going to give Fin full view of my body at a very unflattering angle.

"Trust me. Now come here and ride my face until you come all over my tongue."

I move back down the bed, resisting the urge to try and cover myself from the positioning. I plan on returning the same glorious favour to Fin. Before I make it as far as his hips and his very hard cock to start the process of peeling each layer of clothing off him, his phone goes off.

"Tonight seems to be the night for cock-blocks," I laugh assuming he's going to ignore it and let me get down to business. Then I recognise the ringtone, the same one as last time and I can already see how this is going to play out.

"I'm so sorry, Olivia, if it were any other number, I wouldn't." He reaches over to the nightstand speaking into the phone in a series of one-word answers: "Yes. Understood. When. Where." A one-sided conversation is difficult enough to follow without one side deliberately keeping their answers vague. I already know what Fin is going to say from the look on his face before he even speaks. "I really am sorry. I have to go."

"Now?"

"Yes, now."

I stand up off the bed and grab my dressing gown, pinning Fin with my gaze. I start pacing and then grabbing clothes and throwing them on whatever way I find them. All my questions and hurt from the last time he did this to me quickly bubble to the surface.

"I swear to God, Fintan Kelly if you walk out that door without giving me a reasonable explanation that will be it; I will not listen to your excuses again. I don't care if you show up at work or at my home – we will be done."

Fin stops in his tracks and slowly turns around. "I didn't want to have to bring us down with this yet. It's not pretty and I don't have enough time to try to ease you into this," his hands are shaking as they clench and unclench, "my mother is a functioning, chronic alcoholic and has been for most of my life. It's one skeleton we were ordered to never let out of the closet. She's the reason I moved back up here. She's refusing to go into a facility and needs someone close by to co-ordinate her care. She's also in hospital because according to the phone call I just received she just tried to kill herself."

Chapter Thirteen

'Survival is not so much about the body, but rather
it is about the triumph of the human spirit.'
-Danitra Vance

I slowly make my way back into the waiting room. Fin doesn't hear me so I take the opportunity to watch him. I see no trace of 28-year-old Fin and no sign of the Fin who broke my heart. This is the Fin who was my best friend. His shoulders are slumped in defeat, his fingers arched in front of his mouth as he runs them over his bottom lip. A pseudo-prayer stance made all the more poignant by the movement of his head. He gently moves his head from side to side, but I can't tell if he thinks the conversation with whatever deity it is that likes to mess with us is pointless or if he just can't believe this is happening.

I can't believe it's happening. I always knew Mrs. Kelly liked to have a drink, hell, everyone knew but I never would have thought she was a high-functioning alcoholic. It's not until you witness an event like this that you realise – everyone on this Earth wears a mask and some people wear it best in front of those they love.

I can't begin to imagine the sort of life Fin was having to deal with. A lot of things click into place with this information. Fin never let me into his home apart from one or two meals over the span of several years. Even on those occasions his mother cried off to bed with a headache. He never discussed specifics with me, just as I never told him all the details of my tortures at school. I know my reasons, I didn't want him worrying any more than necessary, it was clear he had enough on his plate. I also knew if he found out at the wrong time he would lose his shit and try to get vengeance for me. I can only guess that his reasons for keeping this from me were similar to mine.

While some things have changed, others remain the same. Fin still takes his coffee pitch-black with two sugars. I set it down on the table in front of him, bringing him out of his melancholic reverie. He looks up at me over his fingers and I lose my breath at the pain in his eyes. This isn't just the pain of finding out your mother might die, but long buried pain that's threatening to take over. Taking a step towards him, unable to speak; not knowing what to say or where to begin, Fin buries his face in my stomach and wraps his arms around the back of my thighs. He doesn't make a sound, the slight tremor in his shoulders is barely noticeable.

I'm not sure how long I've been standing there, running my fingers through his hair, hoping to help alleviate some of his pain when the doctor coming in through the door interrupts us. A tall man with fairly tanned skin and a head full of salt and pepper hair. He has a kind face but you can see in his eyes he's seen more than he wanted to. Fin pulls away and stands, stepping towards the doctor. His hand reaches out behind him and I couldn't resist the magnetic pull of placing my hand in his even if I wanted to.

"Mr. Kelly?" on Fin's nod he continues, "I'm Dr McAuley, sorry for making you wait but I wanted to be sure we had as much information as possible to present to you."

"Just tell me what's going to happen to her."

"You're aware that your mother was brought in as a possible suicide attempt. However, after reviewing her charts and her test results I think it is much more likely that this was an accidental overdose exacerbated by her drinking."

"Most things are exacerbated by her drinking doc, exactly how is this different?"

"The painkillers that she ingested were taken over the space of no more than a few days, but due to the damage to her liver from chronic alcohol abuse it was in too weakened a condition to survive the overdose," he makes direct eye contact with Fin, using this moment to allow the gravity of what he's telling us to sink in, "there's a small possibility that we've caught her just in time. The damage is significant but we need to monitor her closely for several hours and see if her stats plateau, only then will we be able to accurately plot our next course of action. In the meantime, I will assess and review her charts to see if we can put her on the transplant list. However, with her history of alcohol abuse there is a possibility that she won't be approved without guaranteed intervention to stop her drinking. Even then, it's a long shot that they'll approve her."

Fin just nods, as if he'd prepared himself for this possible eventuality a long time ago. "Is she awake?"

"No, we felt it was best to keep her sedated to allow her body a chance to heal from everything. We'll continue to monitor her and bring her fluids and electrolytes back into balance. Unfortunately, it's just a case of waiting and hoping that the damage isn't completely irreparable."

Fin shakes the doctor's hand slowly, morosely, he's already assuming the worst. "Thanks doc, I appreciate all of it." As Fin goes to sit back down, Dr McAuley speaks up again.

"Mr. Kelly, honestly, it's 3am. I won't be bringing your mother out of sedation for at least another 24 hours. Go home, take your wife and get some sleep." After dropping his massive misnomer, he simply nods a tight smile at both of us and makes his way back out.

It never fails to surprise me how busy hospitals are at all times of the day and night. All these people away from their families, working to save lives or make other people's last days on this earth more bearable. Not a bleary eye in sight. A young family comes into the waiting room, holding each other as the sobs of the mother and the son fill the room. The dad doesn't even make an attempt to look stoic, it's just his tears are quieter than his son's.

Fin and I share a look – they need this room more than we do. I grab my coffee with my free hand, as does Fin. "Let's go home." He leads me out of the waiting room and we walk to the car in contemplative silence.

● ● ●

Apparently home means my house, but Fin remains silent the whole journey; his hand firmly grasped around mine. I can feel the fatigue weighing down my body but the adrenaline of rushing to the hospital has my mind still buzzing. Thank God it's the weekend because I would not want to be waking up early tomorrow.

Once we're in the house, we both head straight towards the kitchen. I don't know right now if it's coffee or something stronger I need. "Drink?" My question pulls Fin out of his thoughts, from the look on his face he was running completely on autopilot; God only knows for how long, though it explains the unusually quiet car journey over here.

"Yeah, that'd be great. No, something stronger." He amends when I hold up the jar of coffee.

I pull down the half bottle of Bushmills whiskey which is kept for emergency situations. *I think it's safe to say this qualifies as one.* I pour two fingers for each of us and take them into the front room hoping that Fin will follow me and sit down. He's pacing back and forth that much in the kitchen he's going to wear a hole in the floor.

He follows and joins me on the sofa, where we immediately assume the position – my legs tucked up, my head and body resting on Fin's shoulder with his arm wrapped around me. Fin finally starts relaxing and strokes a hand up and down my side. We sit there in comfortable silence, sipping our whiskey, allowing the tension and adrenaline to slowly drain away. Fin never stops his movements like I'm a human stress ball. If this is what he needs to take the pain away then I'm happy to sit here, the only issue I'm having is trying to control the urge to purr.

"She was always doing stuff like this, ya know." It's clear he's not looking for an answer, so I simply look at him urging him to say whatever he needs to, to make this better for him. "This isn't even the first time she nearly accidentally killed herself. When I was in school she passed out from one or five too many vodkas while making dinner. She slept clean through the fire alarm. The whole of the bottom floor of the house was filling with smoke by the time I came home. The fire was contained inside the oven and I was able to put it out, but it was destroyed and the whole kitchen needed to be repainted. Mum and Dad brushed it off and she joked that she'd been wanting a new kitchen put in anyway," he pauses while taking another sip of whiskey, "I thought she was dead. When I came home, she wasn't moving even though there was all this noise and smoke. I was convinced there was no way she could sleep through that; she had to be dead or dying. For them both to laugh it off like that was typical, they brushed everything under the carpet; until one day my da just couldn't take it anymore. I was already down in Dublin and I got a phone call from him saying he was sorry but without me being there he had no reason to put up with it all anymore." He releases a bitter laugh.

"I'm sorry you had to put up with that. No father should blame his son or use him for reasoning to abandon his wife. She was sick. She is sick." I squeeze his knee to punctuate my point. How dare they do this to him. He was only a kid and they took away the place he should've felt safest. I couldn't imagine coming home every day and not knowing what I was coming home to.

"She's cost me everything that I've loved over the years. I moved down to Dublin because I couldn't look at her for the things she did and the things she made me do. She's cost me so much, Olivia, but no matter what, she's still my mother. I hate the fact that I can't seem to cut ties with her. I moved away to give myself a chance to grow and to forgive her. But I couldn't stay away. I came back because she was getting sicker. She refuses to go into rehab or into care so when she calls, I have to come running because I've no idea what she's done to herself."

"Even phone calls in the middle of the night," I add, pieces starting to fall into place.

With a sombre nod Fin confirms, "Even phone calls in the middle of the night. She'd dropped a glass and cut her hand pretty badly that night. Her blood doesn't clot well because of the alcohol so I had to go over and try to stop the bleeding. She ended up having to go to emergency care to get stitches. That's why I couldn't ring you until later on Sunday."

"And I didn't answer." I feel awful for adding to his burdens by being a bitch and not letting him tell his side of the story.

"You didn't know, Olivia, and to be honest you had every right to be pissed considering how I left things. I gave Mark a very redacted version of events just so I could get in contact with you."

"I'm so sorry, Fin." I show him just how much by taking his mouth in a kiss; hoping it will translate to him just how bad I feel.

"Don't apologise. Don't ever apologise for your feelings. You work so hard for everyone else and never give time for yourself."

Fin places me on my back on the sofa and steals my breath in a kiss that has me grasping at his back, trying to get some traction. Suddenly he sits back on his knees, while keeping his arms between my back and the sofa. The momentum brings me upright and Fin whips me over his shoulder.

At my squeal, Fin lets out a broad laugh, sounding genuinely happy for the first time in hours. "I'm not fucking you on the kitchen table again. This time I'm taking you upstairs so I can make love to you properly and keep you prisoner until we're both completely satisfied." My breath catches at his words but I don't speak. I don't want to call him out on his slip and I don't want to break the spell.

He carries me upstairs practically running and slowly slides me down his body once we're inside the bedroom. Fin doesn't let me move, insists on slowly, reverently undressing me himself, savouring every inch of my flesh with his eyes and his hands.

When we're both naked he lies me down on the bed and hovers over me, holding his weight off me on his forearms. Even his kisses are softer, slower, he has no intention of rushing this, yet I don't doubt that we're both still going to have our world's rocked.

Fin breaks away muttering an oath under his breath, I realise that he's forgotten to grab a condom.

"Fin, I'm clean and I've been on the pill for years," I keep my voice light and even. I've only ever been with Rob so I know I'm clean never mind that I'm tested every time I have my smear done. I trust Fin, and I want to feel as close to him as I can tonight. We've both been through so much, I want that comfort of being with him with nothing between us.

Looking at me with startled eyes, "Are you sure?"

"Are you clean?" At his nod, I reply, "then I'm sure."

The feel of Fin sliding inside me skin on skin, hard on soft, velvet on velvet is divine. We both move slowly, afraid to break the tangible connection, eyes never leaving each other's. The pace picks up but never by much until we both come, crying each other's names into our mouths as we kiss.

Chapter Fourteen

Even the events of this weekend can't seem to bring me down today. My mind occasionally wanders to Fin's mum; how long she's been like this and just what an impact it's had on Fin's life. I can't imagine living my life with that sort of secret. I always knew she had her problems with alcohol but I never once considered she was an alcoholic to the extent I saw yesterday. The rest of the time my mind stays anchored on Fin. Where is he right now, what's he doing, is he feeling this new extra closeness just as much as I am?

The students I pass all look like they're regretting that last day's drinking. It'll be interesting to see who actually makes it to class and who'll be there looking so hungover they might puke. In the lecture hall I'm pleasantly surprised by how many have shown up, most look alive apart from Joanne from my seminar group who's currently lying flat out on her table with a pair of sunglasses covering her eyes.

I may do a big show of dropping my pile of books onto the desk with as much noise as possible, much to the pain of my class, if their groans are anything to go by. Sometimes it's nice being a little bit evil. I launch into my lecture on the different types of love within Pride and Prejudice. Today's focus is on whether Elizabeth Bennet truly loved Darcy.

I can understand where Elizabeth is coming from, she finds it difficult to trust Darcy. She didn't even have a Rob to worry about and muddle everything up even more. The past few weeks have been a whole mess of everything. Trying not to compare Fin and Rob. Trying not to compare old Fin and new Fin. At what point did I stop thinking about getting my vengeance on Fin and start seeing him as a different person?

Thinking back over the past few weeks I can't recall when the changes happened. They were so incremental until they weren't negligible anymore. "'It has been coming on so gradually, that I hardly know when it began.' While Elizabeth quickly succeeds that statement with a joke we can presume there is some truth to her sentiment. She finds herself constantly thinking of Darcy, where he is and what he is doing. He pervades her every thought and feeling until she realises he is part of who she is now. Just as she is part of him." My students scribble away, completely unaware of the epiphany happening behind the lectern. I love Fin. When the hell did that happen? When did I start wondering where Fin was and what he was doing?

No one will ever replace Rob or what he did for me. If I hadn't had Rob and Mark in my life I have no doubt I wouldn't be here now. It's that simple. I'll always owe them my life. But Rob isn't here anymore. I think I've finally accepted that he's not coming back. It gives any happiness I have a bittersweet tinge; but I know that honestly Rob would be first in line to kick my ass for wasting the last two years being so melancholic.

Rob loved me through everything. He supported me through everything, but even with all of that I was never happy with me. I was always trying to lose weight, or do something different with my hair or my makeup. It didn't matter how many times Rob told me he loved me I still felt I needed to make those changes. For some reason when Fin tells me I look beautiful, I believe him. I know he's not saying it to make me feel better or to appease me, he's saying it because he thinks it. I never had that confidence in myself or what Rob was saying to me to feel that before. It's like an iron vice has been released around my chest and I have to turn away from my class because I immediately well up with tears.

The bell saves me from having to explain myself, but of course, Silent Bob is there waiting when I turn back around.

"Are you okay, Miss Murphy?" He looks genuinely concerned.

"I'm fine," *shit, what's his name? Sloane, Stewart? Steven? Steven!* "Steven, thank you for asking. How can I help?"

"I just wanted to talk a little bit more about the different kinds of love in the text." I think he's trying to give me puppy-dog eyes but the poor thing is that stoned that the blood shot whites of his eyes just make him look like he's trying to stay awake.

"Okay, Steven, make sure you call by my office before the seminar at two and sign up for one of my appointment times. Bring your texts with you and we'll see what we can dig up."

"Thanks, Miss Murphy." He shuffles off and I don't know who's more shocked that we just managed to have a conversation, him or me.

$$\bullet \ \bullet \ \bullet$$

Fin and I are meeting for a quick lunch before I have my seminar class. It's going to take everything I have in me not to burst out the words 'I love you' as soon as I see him. I need to plan this carefully, methodically. I need to make sure he isn't somewhere where he'll run as soon as I tell him who I am. Somehow, I need to get him to listen.

The coffee shop is about ten minutes off campus and Fin's already seated and waiting for me. He has my usual chicken and cheese panini waiting for me. The second he sees me he stands and pulls out a chair for me; giving me a quick kiss that still manages to leave me a little breathless. "Hello, beautiful."

"Hi yourself, gorgeous."

"How's your day been?" Fin asks as the server comes over with coffee for both of us.

"Not too bad to be honest. I've one more group seminar this afternoon and then I'm free. How are you doing? You're running on very little sleep, sweetheart."

Fin runs his hands over his face, taking a deep breath and a mouthful of coffee. "I'm okay, tired, but okay. There's no more word from the doctors, all we can do is wait and see if her kidneys start responding."

His hand is warm from the coffee cup when I take it in mine. "I have something for you. I want you to use it and go get some sleep. Then when I get there I'm going to make you dinner and we're going to get through this together."

"Oh and what is it you have for me?" There's a smirk playing at his lips so I've managed to succeed in lightening the mood a little at least. Pulling out the key to my house that I had cut on my way to lunch; I show him the rugby ball keychain with the university colours on it. "I think that ball might be a little small to practice with babe." I snatch the ball back again.

"It's not the rugby ball, you ass. It's the key it's attached to. A key to my house." I'm suddenly starting to feel like I've made this into too big a deal inside my own head. Maybe I should've just left it on the table and been a bit more nonchalant.

"A key to your place?" At my nod he continues, the smile on his face getting wider, "really? That's a huge step, Olivia, are you sure?"

My smile mirrors his, "I wouldn't be giving it to you if I wasn't sure. It's not like you're moving in or anything. It just means that you don't have to wait around for my classes to finish if we're heading out." I shrug my shoulders hoping to alleviate some of the tension. I'm questioning myself now, maybe it is too soon. I shake the thoughts from my head almost as soon as they arrive. I know how I feel about Fin now. The need to know his reasoning for my ill-treatment at school is outweighed by my feelings for him now. I'm not asking him to move in with me, this is just a baby step towards a big step. "Take the key. Go to my place and get some sleep. No one will bother you there. Put on your Do Not Disturb except for the hospital and just get away from everything for a few hours. As soon as I finish my seminar group I'll come back and make us both some dinner."

"Sounds good to me, babe. See you about four, yeah?"

I swallow the huge bite of panini in my mouth. The chicken melting in my mouth, hitting the spot perfectly. "Yep, seminar is over at three thirty so I should be finished up and home by four." Fin manages to inhale his sandwich in four bites. I will never understand how they put that much food away. I wouldn't be able to move after eating that much, that fast.

Fin checks his phone again. "Nothing more from the hospital."

"Then go to my place, get some rest. I'm done here. I'm just gonna head back to work now anyway. You look dead on your feet."

"I'm at least going to walk you back to work, babe. I'm not much of a date if I leave you to make your own way back."

"You can walk me as far as your car, Fin, I'm worried enough about you driving to my place without you walking me to campus and back again."

"Fine, it's a deal but I'm not happy about it."

96

After speeding through my seminar group and hoping they didn't notice I was being a little generic in my discussion commentary, I speed walk to the bus. Making my way home I keep getting some funny looks. I can't say I blame them, if someone was bouncing in their seat, practically vibrating for no outward reason I'd be giving them a wide berth too.

I practically run up my driveway, ready to see Fin and tell him how I feel. I want to show him that I love him, in spite of everything we've been through. I know I'm going to have to handle this delicately, not only am I a blast from his past but I've been lying to him for weeks. At the beginning for nefarious reasons. I can only hope that when I explain where I'm coming from he'll understand; that's if I can get him to listen.

When I get to the door it's still locked, which is weird. I call out for Fin once I'm inside, but it's like he never got here. The only sign of life is that my post is sitting on the end table. I'm practically past it when I look again and see the rugby ball keychain I put on Fin's key sitting on top of the letters. Walking slowly towards the post, as if it's a bomb waiting to blow up in my face, I nudge the key off the top letter and lose all the air in my lungs. The heading on the envelope clearly states *St Ignacious High School.* The scratchy handwriting underneath crossing out my parents' address and replacing it with my own is clearly my mother's. What she didn't scratch out was my name, glaring up at me from the ivory paper, *Elizabeth McKeen. Son of a bitch!*

I've left it too late and now Fin knows who I am, but he doesn't know why. I've no doubt he's assumed the worst. There's no excuse for lying to him this long. Damnit, why couldn't I have realised how I felt before now? I can't bring myself to wish I'd never started this charade because it brought Fin back into my life.

I grab my phone, trying to dial Fin despite the shaking of my hands. It rings off the hook. I try again.

Again.

Again.

He never answers.

Chapter Fifteen

'Lies and secrets, they are like a cancer in the soul. They eat away what is good and leave only destruction behind.'-Cassandra Clare

Two Weeks Later

"If I have to hear Chris Issac sing about the wicked games people play one more fucking time I'm going in there to off her myself. I swear to God!" Mark's voice carries a hell of a lot farther than he realises. You would think that managing to completely fuck up my life would grant me a little bit of wallowing time. Okay, two weeks of wallowing time.

Two weeks of unanswered calls.

Two weeks of unanswered texts.

Two weeks of anywhere I was, Fin wasn't.

For the first time I missed a rugby match by choice. Fin made it clear to Mark if I was there, he wouldn't be. I couldn't risk the entire team for my own stupid mistakes. So I kept my ass at home, eating Doritos and ice-cream.

I've slept-walked my way through my classes. I'm functioning – but barely. Even my students have been giving me a wide berth. I'm emanating a wide array of Do Not Mess With Me vibes.

When you're lying counting the number of shadows on your ceiling, your mind tends to wander. I think that's what makes all of this so much worse. I know this is my fault. I was so hell bent on getting some sort of vindication for the life Fin and the Bitches subjected me to that I lost sight of what was important. Fin was the person I let in after Rob died and I didn't even realise I was doing it. He managed to slowly but surely infiltrate every part of my life in so many different, wonderful and surprising ways. It was like having my old friend back.

I've been dodging any real conversation with Mark and Josie because I don't deserve their pity or their apologies. This wasn't my idea to begin with but I was the fool who decided to go along with it and took it too far. I should have recognised I was developing real feelings for Fin sooner. I know if I'd realised that what I was feeling was real I would've told him the truth sooner. My stupid need for vengeance has cost me the only person I've ever loved before and after Rob.

I don't care what his reasoning was for his behaviour in high school. Spending this time with Fin, I can see he's the same person I loved as my best friend. The same person who was my first love. I'm convinced more than ever that there must've been some reason for what he did. Some unseen outside force. What I don't understand is why he never told me. If he'd just told me, we would've worked something out.

All of this is just speculation. It's all pointless really because I'm not going to get the opportunity to get him to listen to me.

My internal berating is interrupted by a large fist banging against my bedroom door.

"Come the fuck on, Livvy. Get your ass out here. If you're going to insist on self-flagellating, then you're at least going to do it with some bloody alcohol." Ahh Mark, as ever, he's as subtle as a brick through a window. More banging follows, "Now, Livvy or so help me God I will come in there and pull you out myself."

I believe him, the great big oaf would do it too. I peel myself off my bed and shuffle towards the door. My fluffy slipper socks gliding along the wooden floor. They'd help me make an amazing ninja if I wasn't so naturally uncoordinated.

I trudge downstairs begrudgingly, the smell of freshly popped popcorn the only highlight. *God I'm pathetic.* When I reach the bottom step I see an array of junk food spread out over my coffee table and, Jesus Christ, a bottle of Sambuca. This will not end well.

"Now, my bitches, we are here to help Livvy drown her sorrows and maybe also help her find her balls somewhere along the way."

"Hey, I don't have balls!" I mean, come on!

"Oh, we are well aware of your lack of testicular fortitude, but we plan on helping you either find your balls or ovaries of steel."

"That quite literally makes no sense, Mark. Seriously, the next time I'm in your house I want to see your Biology degree. I'm not convinced you didn't send off for it from the back of a cereal packet."

"Hush now, crazy lady, sit that fine ass down and let the drinking commence." He twirls around my living room like he's announcing to an audience. He's lucky he's my best friend because I'm becoming more and more convinced that he's a can short of a six-pack.

"Come over here my love and let us help you drink the worries away." Josie pats the seat beside her on the sofa. But all I can see is where I made love with Fin. Everywhere in this house reminds me of Fin. I haven't been able to eat in the kitchen because all I can think of is Fin taking me on the table.

I plonk myself down beside Josie, tuck my legs up and wrap my arm around my knees. It's as close to the foetal position as I can get while still being technically sitting. Mark hands each of us a shot glass and sits down on the one clear spot of the coffee table – directly in front of where Josie and I are sitting.

"Sláinte."

Jesus, it's burns. This shit never gets any easier to drink. Mark doesn't even give us a chance to catch our breath and he's pouring another round.

"Technically it's nearly Thanksgiving in Canada or America or somewhere, so fuck it let's all toast something we're thankful for." Mark looks on expectantly as if he's just spouted an awe-inspiring haiku. "Fine, I'll go first. I'm thankful for gorgeous redheads and their lack of gag reflex." He just about manages to raise his glass and knock it back without spilling any.

"With that beautiful image emblazoned in our brains; I'm thankful for family and the fact that I'm going to be an auntie." Josie's face splits into a wide grin as she reaches over and closes my mouth which must be hanging wide open at that bombshell. Josie's baby brother has been with his girlfriend since they were fifteen, ten years together and there's still no sign of them getting married. But with Marie pregnant, there's maybe a better chance of Luke actually proposing.

"That's amazing news, Josie! I'm so happy for you." We hug it out, careful not to spill any alcohol and after Mark envelopes her in a bear hug she knocks her shot back.

All eyes are on me, so I guess it's my turn.

"Um, well, I'm thankful for you guys. I don't know where I'd be without you both." My attempt to take my shot is thwarted when Josie and Mark both snort and dismiss my toast in perfect synchronicity.

"There is no way on God's green Earth we are the thing you are most thankful for, Livvy."

"Are you shitting me woman?"

"What? You two are the most important people to me in the world." I seriously don't understand what their issue is.

"Livvy, sweetheart, you know we both love you but we are not the most important people in this world. I want you to listen to me very carefully. I watched you when you first came to college. You were this timid little thing, afraid of your own shadow. You looked like you'd been through hell. It took you months to open up and trust me. I was with you when you started starving yourself and wasting away to nothing. Although I managed to slow you down, you were still hell bent on losing as much weight as possible. I was with you when you met Rob. I was there as you fell in love and Rob tried and failed to help you see what we all saw – an intelligent, witty and beautiful woman. No, don't you dare shake your head at me. As much as I hate Fin for what he did and for being in any way responsible for destroying that young girl that had to move to a completely different school just to be able to live without fear. Him being back in your life, he's managed to do what none of us could. He's got you smiling and laughing and more importantly, I haven't seen you weigh yourself or count a single fucking calorie in weeks. It's not that you're only seeing your worth because of him. It's that he's finally opened your eyes to what the rest of us see all the time."

Josie decides to get in on this mini-intervention, "Ask yourself honestly, when was the last time you had to listen to your meditations or repeat your affirmations? It's like that extra little part of your brain that was always spinning has finally taken a break. I don't know about you, but as your friend and getting to see you so happy within yourself, I think that's worth being thankful for. That's worth fighting for."

With a lack of anything to say I down my drink without a toast and think about everything they've just laid out before me. I think back to my life with Rob. I was happy. I *know* I was. At the same time, I know I wasn't happy with myself. It wasn't Rob's fault and it wasn't mine. Years of sustained abuse messed with my head. I've had enough shrinks tell me that and it's been a painfully slow process gaining and holding onto any self-esteem. Fin took the pressure off. I was so busy focussing on my plan and then enjoying myself and my time with him that there wasn't enough headspace for those thought processes to take up prime real estate. When I wasn't thinking about it and I wasn't looking, those insecurities that normally ate away at my psyche became smaller and smaller. Even now, without Fin in my life they don't hold the same power over me anymore. I know that what was done to me all those years ago had nothing to do with me and everything to do with a group of easily manipulated girls and one in particular that couldn't find any self-worth in herself without stealing it from someone else. I know that after everything I've been through in my life I'm strong enough to sustain this. Now that there's been a turn in the battle I can win the war against my own demons. What I don't want to do is fight this battle on my own. I don't need Fin to be happy, but I *want* him because he makes me happier. It's easier to laugh and not focus on the negative when I have him in my life. It's a life I want to enjoy to its fullest and I haven't enjoyed it as much as I did with Fin in a very long time.

"I need to see him, don't I? I need to swallow my pride, apologise and get him back."

"Fuck yes, you do! Now that is something to toast."

Mark pours another round for everyone. "So, how are you going to do it if he won't meet you and you don't know where he'll be?"

"Oh shit." The realisation of what I'm going to have to do to get Fin back hits me like a freight train, "I'm going to have to go back to school."

Chapter Sixteen

'It is better to die on your feet than to live on your knees.'
- Dolores Ibarruri

My hands slip on the steering wheel that's slick from sweat. I can't believe I'm going to do this. I can't believe I'm actually going to walk into this den of vipers. The drive to the reunion both goes far too quickly and doesn't take long enough.

Alban's Lodge is holding the reunion; it's more than a bit out of the way. The wind whips up the sea so that foam lashes the road in front of me as I drive through the coastal villages on my route. There's nothing between me and the sea than a two-foot basalt wall. The white and black houses to my left face the elements head on, standing unwavering against nature's onslaught. I just hope I can do the same when my time comes to face Fin.

Turning off the coast road I make my way up the winding driveway, Alban's Lodge watching my every movement. The three walls of windows in the function room clear in my memory are now standing, foreboding over the snaking path and the tumultuous sea below. The sheer volume of cars parked outside tell me that there's a reasonable turnout. Given that I've deliberately avoided staying in touch with anyone from school means I'm going in here alone and unprotected.

The event technically started an hour ago and I haven't RSVP'd so I don't have to worry about signing in. The welcome desk outside of the function room is unmanned so I make my way in unaccosted. A wave of heat and Britney blasting out Toxic hits me as soon as I open the door. Almost a hundred of my classmates and their significant others are dotted all around the room. I miss my long hair. It was the perfect way to hide when I was in school. A natural way to blend into the background.

I keep scanning the room trying to find Fin. It becomes clear pretty quickly that

I would be absolutely useless in a covert operation. Several people try to make eye contact with me but I keep running my eyes over the room hoping to catch a glimpse of the body that is so familiar to me now.

My line of sight is obstructed when someone stands in front me. I immediately recognise him as Gavin Quaid. The school football star. He was always with Fiona and the other Stepford Bitches, often egging them on. He even made a point of trying to be my friend at one point just to openly make a fool of me in the cafeteria in front of half the school. Karma is a bitch, who is happy to wait until the time is right. Then, Gavin was fighting women off, his athletic body and good looks buying him a lot more credibility than he deserved. Now, Gavin is already starting to go grey at the temples and his hairline is receding. He's let himself go, his suit ill-fitting and unable to hide his paunch and the sloping of his shoulders. *Looks like someone has been spending more time behind a desk than behind a football.* The thought that the man who relentlessly verbally abused me for being overweight, finally has some insight into what life is like to go around plus-sized, brings a smile to my face. Unfortunately, Gavin takes that smile as an invite to try and crack on to me.

"Well, I'm sure I'd remember a pretty face like yours from school." He adjusts his trousers further up his waist. "I'm sure you remember who I am." His lewd smile does nothing to endear him. It's like all of his personality flaws have slowly but surely made themselves visible.

"Actually, we did go to school together, but if you'll excuse me I'm looking for someone." I can't raise my voice any louder, I feel myself reverting back to my old ways but I can't do anything to stop it. It's like the past twelve years are being stripped away.

"Hey, Blue Eyes, I'm over here." He deliberately puts his face in front of mine. I suppose it's better than my tits which is where his eyes have been locked on to since the start.

"I'm really sorry, but I have to go find my friend." I dip my head down and try to move around him.

As I'm passing by he grabs a chunk of my ass and croaks into my ear, "You're chunkier than I normally go for, but make sure you come find me later. I'm sure you'd rather go home with me than go alone."

I speed forwards, keeping my head down until I know I'm out of his range.

Scanning the room again I catch a glimpse of what I think is Fin sitting at the bar but he quickly disappears behind a red dress. I make my way over for a better look, pushing through the throngs of people, body heat assaulting my senses. I end up slightly off path but when I break through the crowd, closer to the side than the front of the bar, I see the red dress. Casting my eyes up the dress I see long platinum blonde hair being thrown back in a fake laugh. Her long red-tipped fingers are hugging the shoulders of a black suit. She steps back a little and I finally see Fin, sitting on a barstool in front of red dress. He's wiping red lipstick from his mouth, looking up at the blonde. I finally get a good look at her face. The initial stab of seeing Fin with someone else's lipstick becomes a mortal wound when I see that the owner of the red dress is Fiona.

She bends back down to kiss him again. He doesn't even move from the seat, his hand still wrapped around the glass of whiskey on the bar. I'm frozen in place watching the horror show in front of me. Someone bumps into me and I must make some sort of noise. Either from the pain in my foot someone's clown feet just caused or the pain in my heart from watching Fin with the woman who orchestrated making my life hell. Fiona stops trying to eat Fin's face whole long enough to whip around and sneer when she sees me. Fin seems confused for a moment, but his bloodshot eyes focus on me and almost immediately I see the shutters fall behind them.

"Lizzy," he half croaks, half slurs, "what are ya doing here?"

This clearly gives Fiona some sort of green light. She spins around completely, piercing me with her stare. "Oh this is rich. Bessie the Elephant comes back to the herd. I'm surprised the shaking ground didn't alert me to your fat ass arriving."

"Fi," Fin snaps at her, his eyes never leaving mine.

Don't cry, never cry, never let them see you cry. I can't speak. If I speak, I'll cry. I just look at Fin, waiting for something, anything to make me stay.

"Come on, Fintan, let's go. It's a bit too," Fiona gives me a pitying glance up and down, "crowded around here." She takes Fin by the hand and leads him off to one of the corner booths.

It's the final stake to my heart and my cue to leave. I'm not going to stand here anymore; he's clearly made his choice. Apparently my deception was too great and what he felt for me too little.

Our eye contact is broken when he's retreats with Fiona so I turn on my heel and speed walk my way out of there as quickly as possible. If I'm going to cry I'm sure as fuck not going to do it where any of these assholes can see.

How appropriate that as soon as I step outside, the storm that had been threatening finally hits. There's an awning that runs around the whole building so at least I'm not getting soaked. The salty air from the sea is cooled exponentially by the winds from the storm. It's refreshing and gives my senses the shock it needs to stop me crying. It's times like these I wish I smoked. I did try at one point, thinking it would suppress my appetite enough to help me lose weight. All it did was give me one hell of a cough and month of not being able to see Fin except in school because my parents grounded my ass when they found out.

The thought that I've completely fucked things up with Fin leaves me breathless. I'm so angry for lowering myself to their level. My inane quest to prove I had moved on was both pointless and fruitless. The very fact that I wasted time and energy on it in the first place proves that I hadn't moved on. I spent all of ten minutes in that room and managed to revert back to my old ways. *What the fuck is wrong with me?*

I think back to my old life, the girl I used to be. Elizabeth never spoke out of turn, she was always too willing to please; even if that meant causing myself pain or trouble. Instead of it endearing people to her, most saw her as a weak target – a resource to be used and abused. I compare that with the woman I am now. I'm still fiercely loyal and will do whatever I can for my friends but I've learned how and when to say no. All the events in my life leading me to this moment have taught me to be me – no matter what.

If Fin wants to choose that crazy bitch over me then he can. But I'll be damned if I'm going to let him choose her without at least giving him my side of the story. If he still wants her then he can bloody well have her.

With renewed purpose I stride back into the function room. God help any poor bastard that crosses my path. God or karma has a serious sense of humour because only Gavin is stupid enough to cross my path. I don't even let him open his mouth. I channel my confidence, remembering that I am Olivia *fucking* Murphy renowned author, academic and one of the youngest lecturers in BelU history. No strike that, I'm Elizabeth McKeen and I'll be damned if I'm going to let some trumped out, small town, wannabe grope me and walk all over me.

"Listen has-been, before you waste the energy and open your fucking mouth, understand the words that are coming out of my mouth. I do not want you. I didn't want you in school, I don't want you now. And honey, I would say you're too chunky for my tastes but that would be an insult to all the larger people I know and love in my life. I'm Elizabeth McKeen and as God as my witness if you don't get the fuck out of my way right now, I'm going to install my stiletto in your scrotum and release about a decade's worth of anger in your direction." I don't even need to really raise my voice.

I see the colour drain from his face as my tirade continues. His mouth drops open and when I'm finished he takes a step to the side. "Alright, alright. Damn woman, no need to get violent."

I take one purposeful step forward, planning to leave this fuckwad behind and go find Fin before that whore sticks her claws into him any deeper. "You touch my ass again without my express permission and violence will be the least of your problems." With that I leave him in my wake and continue on my quest.

The blonde bitch is practically dry-humping the air around Fin, who still has one hand firmly gripped around his now refilled drink. With a quick glance I notice that her cronies are in attendance too. *Good, I only plan on doing this once, may as well deal with them all in one fell swoop.*

I raise my voice just enough to be heard over the din, but not loud enough to appear angry. I'm not going to give these bitches the satisfaction of seeing how angry I am. I do, however, channel every ounce of anger I have. Anger at my life in school, anger at fate for taking Rob away from me, anger at myself for deceiving Fin, anger at the Stepford Bitches' parents for not doing something earlier to stop their daughters becoming such self-aggrandising bullies, and anger at Fiona for thinking that just because I'm bigger than her she will always have the upper hand and can take whatever she wants, whenever she wants it. "Fin."

Whether it's the volume or tone of my voice, they both stop sucking each other's faces and sit back. Fin just looks at me; I'm assuming waiting for me to speak. Well I won't make him wait long.

"If you're going to make this choice, then I want it to be an informed one. I know what I did was wrong. So wrong on so many levels and I'm not going to attempt to justify it but I am going to explain it. For years you saw what they did to me. Years and years of mental abuse, because that's exactly what it was. Not banter, not girls being girls, it was straight up abuse. And every person watched it happen and did nothing, except you. You were my shelter; you were my safe place. You stood up for me, gave me company when those *people*," I couldn't control the snarl of my lip on that word, even if I wanted to, "had convinced everyone else to never acknowledge my existence. Then you just stopped. No explanation, no apology, no warning. You just stopped, everything. I had no one to turn to, not a single person. Did you know that after you turned your back on me I would go a whole day without a single person speaking or looking at me? From the moment I got on the bus to school until I walked in my front door at home it was as if I were a ghost. A pathetic ghost that wasn't worth anyone's time or effort. You did that Fin. You. You took the one thing that had given me a reason to keep on living and you took it away from me." I'm only just now noticing that we've attracted quite a crowd. Even the DJ has turned off the music. "Every one of you are responsible for what was done to me. You might not have called me names. Or locked me in rooms. But every single one of you stood by and let it happen. You could've reported it. You could've backed me the few times I tried to stand up to them. By standing by you gave them more power than they ever deserved. You gave them the power to make my life a living hell. So, when I got the chance to have my revenge, I took it. I'm not proud of it, but I went through hell for five years in school and I've been through hell the past two years since Rob died. But you managed to make the impossible, possible. You took the hate and rage and heartache that was destroying me and turned it into love. I fell in love with you, Fin. Even after everything you did, I fell in love with you. You finished the job that Rob started. You helped me realise that I could love myself, just as I am. I don't have to be anyone else when I'm with you because I'm enough just being me. I forgive you for turning your back on me. I forgive you for standing me up. I forgive you for joining in on their abuse. But if you can't forgive me, if you can't love me back; then I'll accept that. But know this, Fintan Nicholas Kelly, I loved you then and I still love you now." The rise and fall of my chest is the only movement in the room. Everyone seems to be either staring at me or Fin. I never take my eyes from his piercing hazel; more green than brown, and I don't know if that's good or bad for me. I stand there waiting, hoping that I might've gotten through to him. That he might understand where I'm coming from. The longer I stand there the clearer it becomes that I've pushed him too far. I get no response from him. The only sign of any victory is that Fiona and her crew look contrite. Even though Fin still won't take me back I'm happy that I've maybe made the Stepford Bitches reassess their choices in life. With no answer from Fin I've nothing left to wait for. I turn on my heel and walk away knowing that I'm in a better place than I was a few months ago but I'll never have Fin back in my life.

Chapter Seventeen

'No man chooses evil because it is evil; he only mistakes it for happiness, the good he seeks.'
- Mary Wollstonecraft Godwin

The squealing of my smoke alarm tells me that I've finished cooking dinner. Why I decided to cook a roast for Sunday dinner when it's just me, Mark and Josie I'll never know. That's a lie. I do know, I'm trying to keep myself busy. This past week since I went to the reunion I've done a lot of thinking. It's strange, I feel like I'm in a better place that I have been in a long time. I'm still careful about what I eat but I don't berate myself if I go off diet. I'm aiming now to be healthy, not skinny. I'm happy within myself with no one else having to validate me for the first time since I can remember.

But through it all I'm sad. I miss Fin. I'm thankful that we're on a break from the rugby season for the lead up to Christmas. I don't know what I would do if I had to keep missing rugby matches and not see the team I've been a part of for the past ten years. It's been a week since I finally got to say my piece. I've actually had a few friend requests come through and messages apologising for never having done something. Apparently, the Stepford Bitches had made quite a few people's lives a misery. If we'd only banded together we could've maybe done something about them sooner.

I think about the demons I managed to lay to rest and I feel lighter where the weight of holding onto all of that hate had pulled me down. Yet every time I catch myself smiling it feels bittersweet. I want to be able to laugh and joke with Fin. Dissect what I said and how people reacted. Talk about how our old classmates have changed. Just be in each other's presence and enjoy the comfort of being together in silence, with no expectation to have to fill it. But he's made his bed and now he's going to have to lie in it.

I can't say that I'm happy for him. I don't for a single second think that Fiona will make him happy. Every time I start to feel sad about losing Fin I start to feel angry that he chose that fuckwit over me. At least I can say I went out fighting.

Mark and Josie come blundering in through the door with a couple of bottles of wine. From the colour of their cheeks and the volume of their laughter I'd say they've already had a few drinks before they got here. "Burning again, Livvy?" Mark asks as he comes in and gives me a peck on the cheek.

"Do you want to starve, Mark?" Josie steals the words just before I was going to say them.

"Get in, sit down and shut up if you want fed, Mark."

"Testy, testy." He puts his hands up in surrender as he makes his way to the table.

Josie kisses me on the cheek as she passes by to put the wine in the fridge as Mark sits down.

"Hey, Livvy, who's the lefty?" Mark starts rearranging the cutlery as he asks.

It takes me a second to register what he's asking. When it sinks in, my heart drops and my eyes well. I tip my head back blinking furiously. *Bloody stupid tears.* "Um, sorry Mark, force of habit. Fin uses his cutlery like that." Mark's sad smile of acknowledgement in response brings another swell of tears. I force them back by sheer will power and go back to dishing up our meal.

Just as I place our plates onto the table there's a knock at the door. I curse myself for my heart rate spiking. I've been caught out by this before. My postman thinks I'm mentally unhinged because twice now I let myself get my hopes up and nearly took the front door off its hinges thinking it was Fin.

In the time it's taken me to mentally berate myself for being so foolish, Josie has gone to answer the door.

"Lizzy?"

At the sound of Fin's voice, I drop the spoonful of mashed potato, splattering the table, pots and plates. Just hearing him speak my real name takes my breath from me. I'd resigned myself to never hearing him speak again, never mind actually knowing and acknowledging who I am.

When I turn around I see Fin standing in the doorway. Apart from the several days' worth of stubble covering his jaw and his hair a little messier than usual, he doesn't look like he's taken our separation as hard as I have.

"Fin."

"I think we need to talk, don't you?" His face doesn't belie what he's thinking, but I can't stop myself from hoping that by being here there's a hope that this might work out.

"Yeah, I think that would be best." Mark and Josie make a move to leave, if this doesn't end well I'm going to need them close by. There's only so much heartbreak one person can take.

Fin must read the hesitation on my face, or he knows how this is going to end, because before I can speak he tells them to stay put.

"We can talk in the study," I add and start walking towards the upstairs spare room. I'm stopped by Josie's hand taking mine, "It's okay, Josie, honestly, sit and eat your dinner," I give her hand a squeeze to reiterate my point and shoot her and Mark a tight smile.

The journey upstairs is quick and silent. It's not until we're both inside and the door is closed that I take my opportunity to give my side of the story.

"Look, Fin, I didn't get the opportunity before to say this, but I am sorry, you know."

"Was all of it fake?" Fin appears completely unmoved, he's just standing there stoically, waiting for my answer. I decide to go with the truth. If this is my last hurrah then I may as well go all in, balls to the wall.

"No. I swear it was all the truth. The only lie was one of omission, I didn't tell you my real name. It started out as my pathetic attempt to get some sort of payback for you abandoning me in school. When you appeared back here and didn't recognise me the opportunity just sort of presented itself," at his scoff I keep going, "you have no idea how much you hurt me, Fin. You destroyed me. Without you to help me through the last two years of school I had no choice but to move. I was thinking about it and when you stood me up at prom it was the final nail. I knew I had to leave. I couldn't bear the thought of seeing you every day and not being able to speak to you or touch you or just sit in silence with my best friend." My anger gets the best of me and I end up shouting the last words.

"If I destroyed you so badly and you hated me so much, how can you say you love me?"

I need to sit down, this conversation is taking way more out of me than I thought it would. Running my hands through my hair I try to put exactly what happened into words. "You didn't know who I was so you were your old self again. You from before you went over to the other side. You were sweet and caring and funny. The longer I was around you the more I started to see myself the way you saw me. I started trusting you again and believe me, Fin, that was not an easy feat. I realised when I was spending more of my day thinking about where you were and what you were doing, were you okay, did you miss me too, I knew I was falling in love with you again."

Apparently it's all getting a bit too much for Fin too because he sits on the computer chair facing me. "I never got to tell you I was sorry for what I did to you at prom, and the weeks after. You have to believe me; I didn't have a choice. But by the time I decided that it just wasn't worth it anymore and went to find you, you'd moved schools and your parents wouldn't tell me where. You were staying away during the week and at the weekend your parents wouldn't let me get near the house. Things at home became unbearable and I didn't have my best friend so I decided to run. I transferred down to Dublin and stayed with my Dad's sister and her family."

I can't contain my ironic smile, "So we both moved school and moved in with our aunts. Jesus, even when we weren't talking we were still doing everything together. You still haven't explained why you did that though, Fin. Why you arranged to go to prom with me. Got me to buy a dress, fight against every preservation instinct I had and agree to go. Then just not show up. You wouldn't even answer the phone when I called to make sure you were okay."

Fin leans forward in his seat, briefly taking my hands in his. "You have to believe me; I didn't have a choice. I would *never* have done that to you if I'd had a choice. You know now about my mum. What you don't know is that she's been sick for a very long time. Dad was adamant that no one could ever know. He thought I'd told you once and he grounded me, removed every piece of electronic equipment from the house. He wanted me to understand that because of my actions we were all going to have to suffer. It took me two weeks to convince him I hadn't told you anything. He was ashamed that his wife preferred alcohol to him and he refused to lose face to his neighbours. I never told you but my mum had a serious problem with us being friends. More often than not if she knew I was out with you I would come back to find her in a drunken stupor. It was years before I found out why. Even now I don't entirely understand but I think what started out as a difficult situation for her became more exaggerated the more she drank."

"Why did she have a problem with me? Was it because I was a girl and she was afraid we'd get up to something?"

"Not exactly. Apparently, back in the day, my mum and your dad were a couple. The toast of the school. But when they broke up, your dad moved on too quickly for my mum's liking. He had moved on to your mum, they all went to school together."

"They never told me that!"

"They never told me either. I pieced this together from drunken rants and the minimal information I could get out of my dad. She was pissed he'd moved on so easily so she got her own back by dating an older guy with an accent. My dad. He'd just moved up here for work and my mum thought him being four years older and a working man would put your dad's nose out of joint. This went on for a couple of months, her trying to throw her new relationship in your parents' faces. It didn't work, but before she could break up with my dad she realised she was late. She was about six weeks along and decided she'd rather be with someone she didn't love than try to raise a baby on her own."

I'm trying to work out dates because something isn't right here. Fin is the same age as me and my parents were 25 when they had me.

"She lost the baby Lizzy, about two months after she'd married my dad. I was a drunken accident several years later. After she lost the baby she started drinking more, she swears she stopped while she was pregnant with me, but unfortunately after I was born she went straight back to it. The night of prom I'd had enough of her snide comments about you and your family. She wanted me to be with Fiona because she apparently came from 'good stock'. She'd realised that all those times I'd told her I'd been out with other lads from my class I was actually with you."

I don't know what happened next but I can tell from the look on Fin's face it didn't end well. His struggle is obvious, so this time I take his hands in the hope that they help him get through this and finishing exorcising all of our demons.

"I came downstairs in a tux and when she confronted me about who I was going with I told her the truth. She went on a rampage, destroying everything she could lay her hands on. When she started to quieten I thought I could reason with her but she grabbed a broken bottle and held it to her arm. She swore, she swore she would kill herself if I ever had anything more to do with you. I could tell from the look on her face, Lizzy, she meant it. She meant every damn word. The last three months of school she held that over my head. She would invite Fiona round and try to make nice. Make pretend in her own sick head that this was her life. When I knew she'd cost me you for good, I gave up. I had it out with my dad and packed my things and left. It didn't take long for him to have had enough without me there as a buffer. He never beat her, he never said nasty things to her, but he was never there for her. She checked out through the drink and he checked out emotionally. Our house was where he slept but that was all he did. I don't know if I'll ever be able to forgive them both for the parts they've played in this."

"It doesn't matter now Fin. I fell in love with you before I knew all this. I fell in love with you still thinking you were that callous bastard who turned his back on me. I don't know about you but I won't let them take anything more from me. I loved you when I was 12 years old. I loved you when I was 16 years old, and I still love you now. You've been surrounded by lies and deceit and I don't think I can ever properly express how sorry I am for becoming one of those who lied to you."

"I understand Lizzy, I know you never let me know everything they did to you, but I knew enough how hard me turning on you would be. I thought I was picking the lesser of two evils." He squeezes my hands still tightly wrapped in his.

The thought of him having Fiona in his life and his mother playing house with that bitch shred the last of my remorse. I've apologised and explained my reasoning. But Fin still has some explaining of his own to do. "Well I guess we both have a better idea of where we coming from now, don't we?" I stand up, pacing the floor, strengthening my resolve to do what I need to do next, "I can't put myself on the line anymore Fin and I'm done playing games. So, I'm just going to ask straight out. Did you fuck her?"

It takes Fin a second to register my question, I can see his eyes widen when the penny drops. He's on his feet and stopping my movements with his hands on my shoulders in less than a second. "No," his hands move to my face, forcing me to look in his eyes, acknowledge the truth of his words, "I. Did. Not. Fuck. Her. She's was bitch then, she's bigger bitch now." He steps away from me, pacing his own little segment of the room, fingers locked behind his head. "I was seriously fucking pissed. Before I say anything more, I need you to understand that. I thought all of this was game. That you had been playing me from the start. By the time you'd shown up at the reunion I was already half way drowning in half a bottle of fucking whiskey. Fiona hadn't even come near me until a few minutes before you'd shown up. She was there, she was making her intentions really fucking obvious. I was hurting darling, I was falling in love with you too and it had all been ripped away from me by lies again. I flaunted her in your face and I know that. At the time I'd thought you just came to get one last stab in. Then, when you came back and poured your heart out to me, in front of everyone who'd hurt you" he shakes his head, "I tried to go after you, but you'd already left. I called for a ride home and finished my bottle of whiskey there, alone."

"That was a week ago Fin. For a week, every time I closed my eyes I was tormented with the images of you and her together. Why come by now?" All the pain of this last week could have been so easily avoided.

"I needed that time Lizzy. I know it's time we'll never get back and I wish I hadn't, but I needed to be sure of my own feelings. I had been running under the assumption you were playing me." Fin stalks towards me and takes me by the hands. "When I realised you weren't I needed to step back and take stock of everything's that gone on. I spent some time with my mum, it looks like they've managed to catch her just in time. She's still sick and will be for a long time. We hashed some things out. It's still awkward as all hell but we're talking, actually talking, for the first time in as long as I can remember. The whole time we were apart my mind was never far from you," Fin's eyes have been trained on our entwined hands but at this he looks up. I can see the sheen of tears in his eyes ready to fall but I don't know what's behind them. "Do you honestly think now that I have my best friend back in my life I'm ever going to get let anyone steal you from me again? Silly darling, you're never getting rid of me."

Epilogue

Fin

Ok ladies, before we go any further I'm gonna need ya to put down your pitch forks. I'm only going to explain this once more. I was drunk. Hammered. Blotto. Shit-faced. I was hurting, thinking that the girl I was in love with had played me. If I hadn't been drunk I wouldn't have gone near Fiona with a ten-foot pole. Even I can see that she's a stone cold bitch.

It's been six months since Lizzy and I hashed everything out. Things have been good. I got to see her parents again. There was a serious amount of confusion when her mum found out that I was the boyfriend. Also, to say she was pissed when she found out what Lizzy did, would be an understatement. I'm not going to lie, it hurt me at the time. Taking that time apart was what I needed. I'd spent two weeks nursing the hurt, cradling my anger and feeding it, mostly with whiskey. That week after the reunion was one of the hardest I've had. Lizzy had already lied to me once, over several weeks, and I honestly wasn't sure how genuine she was. She's a better liar than I ever thought possible. Every time I tried to think through our weeks together it was tainted. It's impossible to be sure of yourself when you have double guess everything you've been told.

But every time I doubted her feelings, and in turn then, my own; I remembered the look on Lizzy's face in that reunion. Not the first time, thinking of the pain marring her features and unconcealed hurt on her face when she walked in and saw with that tramp. I can't think of it. It rips at my own heart. I should've realised then she was genuine. That second time, she was so determined, so fierce. You could see the truth radiating from her, I could easily imagine the chains she was freeing from around her soul. I envy her that. The two people I still harbour my anger for will never know the extent of the damage they've done to my life. Dad is still AWOL, mostly likely shacked up with someone half his age. Mum, mum is doing better. I haven't inflicted meeting her again on Lizzy, it'll be some time before that happens. She's been in rehab a couple of months now and it looks like it might actually stick. Constant disappointments have taught not to get my hopes up. Lizzy's hoping for the best though. Even now, after being repeatedly let down by life she's still hopeful. She doesn't even realise how much of a gift that is. Plenty of other people would've caved by now, but not my Lizzy. She's as ferocious as she is adorable.

• • •

I wash the last of the shaving foam off my face and apply a healthy amount of aftershave. Enough to entice, but no so much it overwhelms. It's a fine balancing act. I don't ever want to be in a position where I take Lizzy's attraction to me for granted. When I round the corner to our bedroom, a pronoun I'm still getting used to using, I thank God for my timing because I've caught Lizzy right in the middle of pulling up her stockings. Stalking over so she can't hear me, I run my hand along her leg and help her pull her stocking up. Her little jump at the contact of my hand on her thigh gives me the perfect opportunity to bury my face in her neck. I love the access I have to her neck with her hair short like this.

She's wearing a dress that's the colour of black cherries and wraps around her curves like she's a treat only I get to unwrap. Which is exactly what I'm going to do to her when I get her home. I adjust myself, subtly, tucking my getting harder by the second cock down along the leg of my boxers. Lizzy's hand cupping me and squeezing lightly, tells me I wasn't as subtle as I thought I was.

"Don't worry Fin, you'll get to put it to good use later," she leans up on her tiptoes and kisses along the underside of my jaw. She's really not making my situation any easier. If I look down at the right angle while she kisses my neck I can see the black lace of her bra, which is making a valiant effort to control those supple breasts of hers that I love so much.

"Is that a promise?"

"I have to give my champion his treat don't I?" She steps away and starts adjusting her earrings before slipping into her shoes. She still doesn't really wear heels but her shoes tonight have enough of a heel to curve her calves and make me want to run my teeth up them with the stockings still on.

The blast of a horn downstairs tells us that it's time to go. The rugby season is officially over so the entire team is heading out for a slap-up meal, drinks and maybe even a bit of dancing. Thankfully, for me, my co-ordination on the pitch also translates to the dance floor, so I'm not as liable to make a fool of myself as some of our players.

We eventually won the rugby league. It was close, closer than I would've liked but we got there in the end. The university is still trying to stall on the funds for the new centre, but Lizzy isn't giving them much of an option. She's planned enough articles about the whole shady business to keep Mark and I in our jobs for months. Not that I need the security. With mum in rehab I'm not really needed up here as much as I thought I would be. That was our first real argument. I don't count the reunion because we'd technically broken up. Lizzy thought I was putting my career on hold to stay up here and didn't want me to stay out of pity. But at the same time she clearly didn't want me to leave either. I wanted to stay as much, if not more, for her than for my mum and there are plenty of photojournalistic opportunities in Northern Ireland. I managed to convince her that I really, *really* wanted to stay up here by refusing to let her out of bed for twenty-four hours.

That's also how I ended up moving in with Lizzy. I was running on a six-month contract in my place. Since we'd decided I was staying up North I was going to have to either buy a house or extend my contract. Living with Lizzy is interesting to say the least. It was even more interesting when we forgot that Mark had a key and he walked in on us christening the coffee table.

So now, we take the summer off to rest and relax. The next season is going to be just as tough; defending our place as champions and fighting for the funding that is rightfully ours. Before all that though I get to take my girl out, wine her, dine her and well you know the rest.

Acknowledgements

The End, I honestly never thought I'd get to the point where I typed those words. I have so many people who, one way or the other, helped get me to this point. I have to thank my husband, kids, my mum and my two sisters who gave me time to actually put pen to paper and then fingers to keyboard.

My PA, Serena, who deals with my crazy and random gifs with little to no alcohol. She is my sounding board, my voice of reason and one of the most honest, sweetest and hard-working people I know.

Laura and Lauren. Where do I even start? Without you two Robbed wouldn't exist. Our conversations and random voice messages are what have kept me sane. I don't know if I'm ever going to be in a position to thank you both properly.

Eileen, the first person in the book world who ever read Robbed, when it was nothing more than a prologue and 3,000 words. Who gave me the confidence to keep going.

Rose, my crazy-ass personal cheerleader. I love you. Bouncing ideas off you, getting excited when another idea hit and having you there to keep me going. I'm proud to call you friend.

Jacqui, my multi-graduating friend. My non-book world confident. You get to be my devil's advocate because I know you will never steer me wrong. We've been friends for twenty years, we better have a fuck load more than twenty still ahead of us.

Adriane, your enthusiasm is why this book got past the first five chapters. If I ever have to get trapped in the back of a dark moving van, I want it to be with you.

My editor, Stacey. Woman, how you managed to stay sane through my stressing, poor use of end punctuation and grammar nazi ways, I will never know. Thank you for making Robbed indescribably better.

Helena, you have shaped the author and person I've become. I will be eternally grateful for the precious time you've given me. You are one of the most amazing, sweet and funny people I know.

Sebastian, you are the reason this book finished. Inspiration comes in the most random of ways; even hashing out plot points over a plate of pasta, in a city neither of us lives in.

Sarah, Christina, Lauren, Angy, Elaine, Alecia, Jennie, Amanda, Elizabeth, Kristina, Brandi, Veronica, you all were my first friends in the book work and you're a part of my family. #hustlersunite

To all the authors I've come to know as a reader and blogger who've helped me in so many ways. From talking me through freak outs, providing professional opinions on covers to answering an email from a random girl who wanted to know where to start in putting her ideas onto paper. Debra, Shannon, Katherine, Sloane, Celia, CJ, SL, Ruth and Julia, thank you.

The bloggers who took a chance on a debut author who set out 2 years ago to write a dark and twisty novel full of angst and ended up with a romantic comedy- THANK YOU. I can't say that enough, you make the book world go around. Without you this book would've released with a whimper.

I'm sure I've forgotten someone, no matter how many times I've gone over this. To anyone who has been a part of my life in this book world, whether you know it or not you've all played a part in supporting me and bringing this book to life.

Musical inspirations for Robbed

Metallica
King Nothing
Hero of the Day
For Whom the Bell Tolls
No Leaf Clover

Alanis Morissette
You Oughta Know

Ben Haenow
Second Hand Heart

Linkin Park
In The End

Meredith Brooks
Bitch

Chris Issak
Wicked Game

About the Author

CL Sayers is a debut novelist from the UK. She writes under a pen name for professional reasons. She lives at home with her husband, 2 kids, an asshole cat, an easily confused turtle and an ever-changing rotation of fish.

She is a proud coffee addict, Whovain, Xphile and all round nerd.

You can stalk her and keep up with her shenanigans and new releases here:

www.clsayers.com

www.facebook.com/clsayersauthor

http://www.amazon.com/author/clsayers

www.twitter.com/clsayersauthor

www.instagram.com/clsayersauthor

www.pinterest.com/clsayersauthor

www.ingramcontent.com/pod-product-compliance
Lightning Source LLC
Chambersburg PA
CBHW060440130626
46555CB00005B/2437